YOU ARE HERE

The
WriteGirl
Journey

www.writegirl.org

A WriteGirl Publication

ALSO FROM WRITEGIRL PUBLICATIONS

No Character Limit: Truth & Fiction from WriteGirl
Intensity: The 10th Anniversary Anthology from WriteGirl
Beyond Words: The Creative Voices of WriteGirl
Silhouette: Bold Lines & Voices from WriteGirl
Listen to Me: Shared Secrets from WriteGirl
Lines of Velocity: Words that Move from WriteGirl
Untangled: Stories & Poetry from the Women and Girls of WriteGirl
Nothing Held Back: Truth & Fiction from WriteGirl
Pieces of Me: The Voices of WriteGirl
Bold Ink: Collected Voices of Women and Girls
Threads
Pens on Fire: Creative Writing Experiments for Teens from
  WriteGirl (Curriculum Guide)

IN-SCHOOLS PROGRAM ANTHOLOGIES

Ready for the Next Chapter: Creative Voices of the WriteGirl In-Schools Program
No Matter What: Creative Voices from the WriteGirl In-Schools Program
So Much To Say: The Creative Voices of the WriteGirl In-Schools Program
Sound of My Voice: Bold Words from the WriteGirl In-Schools Program
This is Our Space: Bold Words from the WriteGirl In-Schools Program
Ocean of Words: Bold Voices from the WriteGirl In-Schools Program
Reflections: Creative Writing from Destiny Girls Academy
Afternoon Shine: Creative Writing from the Bold Ink Writers Program at the
  Marc & Eva Stern Math and Science School
Words That Echo: Creative Writing from Downey, Lawndale and Lynwood
  Cal-SAFE Schools
The Landscape Ahead: Creative Writing from New Village Charter High School
Sometimes, Just Sometimes: Creative Writing from La Vida West and
  Lynwood Cal-SAFE Programs
Everything About Her: Creative Writing from New Village High School
Visible Voices: Creative Writing from Destiny Girls Academy
Now That I Think About It: Creative Writing from Destiny Girls Academy
Look at Me Long Enough: Creative Writing from Destiny Girls Academy

"*Pieces of Me* is a riveting collection of creative writing produced by girls and women with enormous talent. On every page you'll encounter fresh voices and vibrant poems and stories that pull you into these writers' worlds, into the energy of their lives."

– **Vendela Vida, author,** *Away We Go, Let the Northern Lights Erase Your Name*

AWARDS FOR WRITEGIRL PUBLICATIONS

2013 Silver Medal, Independent Publisher Book Awards: *No Character Limit*
2013 Winner, IndieReader Discovery Awards, Anthologies: *No Character Limit*
2013 Honorable Mention, Eric Hoffer Award, Young Adult: *No Character Limit*
2013 Finalist, Next Generation Indie Book Awards, Anthologies: *No Character Limit*
2013 Honorable Mention, San Francisco Book Festival, Anthologies: *No Character Limit*
2013 Honorable Mention, Paris Book Festival, Anthologies: *No Character Limit*
2012 Finalist, Beverly Hills Book Awards, Anthologies: *No Character Limit*
2012 Winner, USA Best Book Awards, Anthologies: *No Character Limit*
2012 Runner-Up, Great Southwest Book Festival, Anthologies: *No Character Limit*
2012 Runner-Up, London Book Festival, Anthologies: *No Character Limit*
2012 Winner, Los Angeles Book Festival, Anthologies: *No Character Limit*
2012 Runner-Up, Southern California Book Festival, Anthologies: *No Character Limit*
2012 Honorable Mention, Eric Hoffer Award, Young Adult: *Intensity*
2012 Winner, International Book Awards, Anthologies, Nonfiction: *Intensity*
2012 Winner, National Indie Excellence Awards, Anthologies: *Intensity*
2012 Runner-Up, San Francisco Book Festival Awards, Anthologies: *Intensity*
2012 Runner-Up, Paris Book Festival Awards, Anthologies: *Intensity*
2011 Finalist, ForeWord Reviews Book of the Year Awards, Anthologies: *Intensity*
2011 Honorable Mention, Los Angeles Book Festival, Anthologies: *Intensity*
2011 Winner, London Book Festival Awards, Anthologies: *Intensity*
2011 Honorable Mention, New England Book Festival, Anthologies: *Intensity*
2011 Finalist, USA Best Book Awards, Anthologies, Nonfiction: *Intensity*
2011 Winner, International Book Awards, Anthologies, Nonfiction: *Beyond Words*
2011 Winner, National Indie Excellence Awards, Anthologies: *Beyond Words*
2011 Finalist, Next Generation Indie Book Awards, Anthologies: *Beyond Words*
2011 Finalist, Independent Book Publisher Awards, Anthologies: *Beyond Words*
2010 Finalist, ForeWord Reviews Book of the Year Awards, Anthologies: *Beyond Words*
2010 Winner, London Book Festival, Anthologies: *Beyond Words*
2010 Winner, National Best Book Awards, USA BookNews, Poetry: *Beyond Words*
2010 First Place, National Indie Excellence Awards, Anthologies: *Silhouette*
2010 Winner, New York Book Festival, Teenage: *Silhouette*
2010 Winner, International Book Awards, Anthologies: *Silhouette*
2010 First Place, National Indie Excellence Awards, Anthologies: *Silhouette*
2009 Winner, London Book Festival Awards, Anthologies: *Silhouette*
2009 Finalist, ForeWord Reviews Book of the Year Awards: *Silhouette*
2009 Winner, Los Angeles Book Festival, Nonfiction: *Silhouette*
2009 Winner, National Best Book Awards, USA Book News, Anthologies: *Silhouette*

2009 Silver Medal, Independent Publisher Book Awards: *Listen to Me*
2009 Runner-Up, San Francisco Book Festival, Teenage: *Listen to Me*
2009 Winner, National Indie Excellence Awards, Anthologies: *Listen to Me*
2009 Runner-Up, New York Book Festival, Teenage: *Listen to Me*
2009 Finalist, Next Generation Indie Book Awards: *Listen to Me*
2008 Finalist, ForeWord Reviews: *Listen to Me*
2008 Winner, London Book Festival Awards, Teenage: *Lines of Velocity*
2008 Honorable Mention, New England Book Festival, Anthologies: *Lines of Velocity*
2008 Grand Prize Winner, Next Generation Indie Book Awards: *Lines of Velocity*
2008 Winner, National Best Book Awards, USA Book News: *Lines of Velocity*
2008 Silver Medal, Independent Publisher Awards: *Lines of Velocity*
2008 Honorable Mention, New York Festival of Books Awards: *Lines of Velocity*
2007 Finalist, ForeWord Magazine: *Lines of Velocity*
2007 Honorable Mention, London Book Festival Awards: *Untangled*
2006 Finalist, ForeWord Magazine: *Untangled*
2006 Winner, National Best Book Awards, USA Book News: *Untangled*
2006 Notable Mention, Writers Notes Magazine Book Awards: *Nothing Held Back*
2005 Finalist, Independent Publisher Awards: *Pieces of Me*
2005 Finalist, ForeWord Magazine: *Bold Ink*

WriteGirl Publications

Los Angeles

YOU ARE HERE: The WriteGirl Journey

Publisher & Editor	Keren Taylor
Associate Editors:	Erica Blodgett
	Cindy Collins
	Allison Deegan
	Rachel Fain
	Glenda Garcia
	Kirsten Giles
	Connie Ho
	Anna Mkhikian
	Anne Ramallo
	Diahann Reyes
	Marlys West
	Terry Wolverton
	Sandy Yang
Art Director:	Keren Taylor
Book & Cover Design:	Sara Apelkvist
Printing:	Chromatic, Inc., Los Angeles

ISBN 978-0-9837081-2-4

FIRST EDITION
Printed in the United States of America

Orders, inquiries and correspondence:
WriteGirl Publications
Los Angeles, California
www.writegirl.org
info@writegirl.org
213-253-2655

ACKNOWLEDGEMENTS

We, at WriteGirl, want to give a "shout out" of gratitude to the many individuals and organizations that make up the wonderful community reflected in this book. Thank you, thank you, thank you!

Thank you to every member of WriteGirl for making *YOU ARE HERE: The WriteGirl Journey* possible. Each spring, the book production team is happily inundated with a barrage of submissions from WriteGirl teens and mentors, all eager and excited to include their original stories in the pages of our latest anthology. Poetry, prose, songs and excerpts from novels and screenplays arrive to us in a flood of email, snail mail and hand delivery by WriteGirl teens. Some pieces are written in a flash, from beginning to end, at a WriteGirl workshop; others are developed over several weeks or even months of mentee-mentor writing sessions at coffee shops, libraries and dozens of fun and inspiring locations throughout Los Angeles. WriteGirl pens move around the clock, through frenzied days and sleepless nights, creating stories that reflect the lives of the girls who share them. Some pieces have been inspired by dreams, a memory or even a favorite food. Others delve into family life and social life, the way things are and the way things will be. Always, each piece reflects a unique viewpoint infused with a healthy dose of creativity.

Thank you to our WriteGirl parents. We appreciate everything you do to make sure that your daughters get to be part of our workshops and mentor-mentee sessions, as well as the support you give them at our public readings and on the home front. Your contribution to their WriteGirl experience is invaluable.

Thank you, WriteGirl volunteers, for your commitment and participation. You are the supportive, safe and creative container that holds the girls so that they can freely express their perspectives, cultivate their voices and share their work. We thank you for your generosity, talents, expertise and time.

ACKNOWLEDGEMENTS, CONT.

To our friends and supporters, thank you for helping sustain WriteGirl, year after year. You make it possible for us to grow our programming, network and partnerships.

Thank you to the WriteGirl book team of editors, proofreaders, callers and production assistants. Your long hours, late nights and lengthy conversations helped pull all the pieces together to create this new book, in record time, and with care for the tiniest details.

Thank you to Sara Apelkvist for cover and book design – we are very grateful for your many years of contributions. Your very reliable creativity and precision makes this book shine.

Finally, thank you to our teen writers. Your willingness to explore different genres, participate in the workshops, meet regularly with your mentors, sit down and write, then read your work out loud, even as you juggle the extracurricular activities, school work and pressures of being a teenager, is testament to your courage, commitment and tenacity. The world is a better place because you dare to express yourselves and share your journeys with all of us.

You Are Here: Table of Contents

4. Grandma and Pumpkin *Family*

5. Dance Until the Moon Dims *Sleep & Dreams*

6. Her Voice *Viewpoints*

20. This Is WriteGirl

Write to discover yourself.

Foreword

Sometimes when I browse current fiction or movies, I get angry because I see so many stories in which girls are reduced to pretty princesses, passive victims waiting for someone to rescue/educate/enlighten them or do their hair. I'd love to put this anthology into the hands of everyone in the world so they could have a better model of what girls and women are like, and what they can accomplish.

I started volunteering with WriteGirl in its first year, and from the staff to the volunteers and mentors to the girls themselves, I can assure you this is one kickass tribe of women who are fully capable of anything they set their minds to. We were a small group sitting on the floor of Keren's house, figuring out what kind of mentoring we should provide for our first crop of girls. Twelve years later, WriteGirl has sent hundreds of girls out into the world with the confidence that comes from having had their work read, supported and published, not to mention the benefits of having a personal relationship with a professional woman writer. My mentee was a sophomore in high school when I met her; now she's a college graduate beginning her own career as a writer. I continue to mentor her and hope to see her name on a screen or a book cover soon, because I know that the women she writes about are going to be just as strong, resourceful, creative and courageous as she is.

I encourage you to take the time to savor the pieces in this book – you are getting a first look inside the heads of the women who will be shaping our culture in a few years. Note a few things: they are confident and unashamed of emotion; they are powerful and compassionate; they are intelligent *without* arrogance and full of joy and curiosity. They do not put up barriers between people, they tear them down.

They are not in need of rescue, or a makeover.

They are not alienated: They are connected, to each other, to their mentors, and now, through this book, to you. And they are not powerless: They are powerful, through their words. They are here. You are here. Together.

– **Christina Lynch, television writer and co-author of** *City of Dark Magic* **and** *City of Lost Dreams*

Introduction

Community is a difficult thing to cultivate, especially in Los Angeles. We are spread out. We like our individual cars, environments... electronic devices. But every WriteGirl event is a special opportunity for connection, conversation, debate and creativity – in-person, live, now. We ask girls and women to be present, and they have responded enthusiastically, leaving cell phones aside, sometimes for hours at a time! We are grateful for our partnerships with so many of the city's most prestigious artistic institutions such as Walt Disney Concert Hall, the Autry Museum, the National Center for the Preservation of Democracy and the Academy of Motion Picture Arts & Sciences. They give WriteGirl absolutely fantastic settings for our workshops and events, as well as windows to inspirational artists and art. They connect us to the world beyond Los Angeles.

We are all influenced by the journeys of others. Personally, I have been moved, shaken and inspired by recent world events, and most intensely by those involving women. They have deepened my passion and urgency for the work we do here at WriteGirl in helping girls discover and raise their voices. We always keep it fun, fresh and creative, but at its core, WriteGirl is a rare and vital pathway for girls to find their way forward, to grow confident and clear in who they are, what they believe and how their ideas and choices matter, in their families, communities and in the world.

We have seen how countries have claimed their independence in the capital city's town square. Let people gather and there is power there. WriteGirl is that kind of a vital gathering place for girls - a sort of town square for girls to connect with other girls, to meet accomplished women and be inspired, a place to stand up for their ideas and ideals and most importantly, to celebrate their own unique voices and identities. Our group chant, "Never underestimate the power of a girl and her pen," reminds us of why we are here, together, and all of the important writing that there is still to be done.

The journey of WriteGirl is not just in capturing the electricity of love in a poem, or crafting an anthem around a memorable moment, or painting a portrait with words – yes, you'll find these and many other styles and stories inside this book, but what you might not be able to see, in any font or stanza, what you might not hear, in any low tone or bold melody, is what happens on the inside to girls when they are given the space, time and support to just be themselves, to say what they feel, and to think about what they might want to do, give and be, all the while surrounded by creative and kind women.

The journey of WriteGirl is partly here, in the pages of this 12th anthology, but all over the world, there are growing numbers of former WriteGirl members with unbridled creativity, compassion, curiosity and courage who are studying, working and leading projects in more diverse places and on more vital issues than you can imagine. So as you experience *YOU ARE HERE: The Journey of WriteGirl,* remember that it is as much about where we are now as it is about where we are heading.

– Keren Taylor, Executive Director and Founder

1

REGRET COMES OVER AND COOKS FOR ME SOMETIMES

Teen Life

KATE JOHANNESEN, AGE 18

I wrote this at the Nonfiction Workshop. The prompt I answered was, "Are you in a metaphorical cage? How can you escape?" I hope other girls will be able to relate to it when they read it.

Paradox of a Woman Unleashed

I am a woman. At least, that's what they say. I am 18 now. An adult. Responsible. I can make my own decisions from now on. Right?

I was raised in a fish tank – a spacious one filled with colors and light and opportunities; everything I loved, all the people I loved and plenty of good food. Growing up in this tank, I was happy. But the closer I got to where I am now, the more I couldn't help noticing all that lay beyond the safety of my four solid glass walls. I saw cool kids I knew I could never hang out with; concerts I knew I could never attend; boys I knew I could never kiss. The allure of the outside world was almost irresistible; I longed to gather the strength to jump out of the tank and explore what I had never known.

Now I have finally reached that point. In a few months, my parents will escort me out of the tank and into the unknown in some sort of ritualistic procession. I will be going off to an art school in San Francisco. I will finally be living my dream. But I wonder…am I ready? My whole life, I've been sheltered. My whole life, my parents have been there to hold my hand and guide me. What will I do without them? What will I do without the comfort of what I've always known? I'm afraid going to college will be a leap into the void – what if my ultimate dream…becomes a terrifying nightmare?

For most fish, when they throw themselves over the edge of their tank, they die. I can only hope that there will be water, food, color and love on the outside, too.

JAMAI FISHER, AGE 17

Re: My Feelings

Dear My Feelings,

I miss you. I miss the way you helped me make decisions and taught me to cope with the decisions I did make. I used to have so many of you to keep me company, but now it seems most of you are gone. I mean some of the gang still sticks around.

Regret comes over and cooks for me sometimes. Or sits me between his legs and brushes my hair. He also comes over to watch movies in sweatpants and a T-shirt but only when Lonely brings the ice cream.

I drive past Happiness, too, sometimes. Walking down the street with her cute figure and long hair, eyes sparkling in the sun.

I call Pride when I can't figure out what to wear. She has me looking real good when I go out on dates with Self-Esteem. Love keeps calling me, too, but I ignore his calls 'cause every time I talk to him I always go over my minutes and gotta pay for it.

So, Feelings it would be nice to see you again sometime. Maybe we could kick it.

And P.S. When you hit me up can you try not to call on a blocked number so I know it's you?

I wrote about a kid at my school who intrigued me, but whom I knew nothing about.

Chance (That Was Close)

A connection so inexplicable
it makes me breathless.
just to say hello,
and then my head is reeling from the impact
of two like minds colliding;
the only experience of its kind.
As your eyes turn towards me
your gaze swings dangerously
with the powerful force of a sledgehammer.
SLAM. Our eyes meet.
SLAM. Our paths lock.
SLAM. Is that you or am I having a heart attack?
SLAM. The whole world can hear it.
SLAM. SLAM. You're closer, coming. SLAM.
SLAM.
And then
the "hey"
an exchange I remember
for the rest of the day.
The effect you have on me is bizarre
ridiculous
But in the end, I can't help it. It seems silly, really.
Because after all
we hardly know each other
right?

LYNA MORENO, AGE 15

I started off with a phrase I really liked (which is the first sentence of this piece), and I went on from there.

From My Point of View

There was something about him. His teeth were perfectly straight, his lips a typical pink, but when added together, his smile was never quite right – like a recipe gone wrong. The bald patch on his head was as if someone shaved a spot in a daisy field. His beady eyes reminded me of spider eyes that sent goose bumps down my arms. You never knew what direction he was staring at, you just knew he was staring at you. He wore ties with cartoon bananas, dancing leprechauns, or, one time, even hundreds of miniature ties in neon colors. With that I knew he lacked fashion sense. And common sense. And any sense.

And right now, I sat in his office forced to look at his stupid orange fedora, with a fox patterned lining and plum feathers. He had pictures of his beastly wife sunbathing in what could only be assumed to be Hawaii. His desk was filled with trinkets such as a NASA snow globe, a giraffe lamp, a weird alligator back scratcher and some type of laser pen. What was pleasant to look at was the poster of Channing Tatum that hung behind him. Although, he could never be anything like him, I wasn't going to be the one who told him and got the poster taken down. It was the only thing that I looked forward to whenever I was sent to his office.

He sat and stared at me for a few moments. Was he even thinking about me or was he just dozing off into space? He combed his mustache quietly and didn't respond to the huge stacks of paper on his desk that waited for his approval. How in the world did they think he was a good principal?

After working with my incredible mentee for four years – through both wonderful and tumultuous times – I finally get to see her graduate and move on to college. This poem is dedicated to her.

Change of Address

In this box I pack you
All of your most essential needs
A roll of quarters for laundry
A string of lights for your room
A pink, sparkly album for your photos

But I will also gently place on top
The memories of our time together
The book of blank pages that soon burst
With adventures and heartache
The quiet sadness that soon evolved
Into rambunctious maturity
Empty coffee cups, rambling text messages
Soggy tissues and tragic heroines
Who finally find their happy endings

In this box, I hope you also tuck away
All that you have earned for yourself
A gold-emblazoned certificate
A badge of undeniable courage
A resilient spirit that will never fail you

KATHRYN CROSS, AGE 14

I wrote this piece after not making the volleyball team.

Joy

Sadness. It's that feeling when you feel as though the whole world has turned on you and all you want to do is just ball up and cry and have someone tell you it's going to be okay, even though you know it won't be. It's that feeling where you just feel completely empty inside, as though someone just sucked all your being out of you and you become nothing but a worthless lump. It's that feeling where you know that the world is moving around you but it's not taking you with it.

But then you see all of your friends and family around you and the beautiful flowers, sky and small, burden-free creatures that surround you, bringing a new perspective and rationality to your eyes. And you suddenly feel a slight amount of happiness when you realize that things always get better. It may not be the way you expected, but things always get better. Better than the way it was before you were overwhelmed with this sadness. And then you just feel like talking in a British accent or dancing around the room and hugging everyone you see. You suddenly realize that not only did things *get* better, they *are* better. And now you're just bursting with this new feeling. Joy.

I opened my notebook and picked a random piece for the WriteGirl Editing Workshop. It turned out much more concise and fluid than the original.

Anticipating Nirvana

I eat graham crackers and study flashcards for the SAT.
Mom's sock is still on my desk. There's
Chaos in Syria, chaos in North Korea. Chaos here.
The toilet leaks in the bathroom, a nook in the hall:
a void opens, growling, then back to sleep for just a minute, only to roar again.
Even the plumber couldn't fix it.

We join clubs. We accumulate accomplishments for resumes.
I give myself a basketball, something to do. But
at the end of the game, I'm back to distracted meditation.
Outside I practice my hobbies, my sport. Outside I point to the college I want.
Inside I ridicule, cross-examine, interrogate.
Inside I doubt this counterclockwise rollercoaster.
The g-force won't ever wake us from our coma together!
I laugh, but can't remove the feeling to measure it and save it for later
like the quantum atom that ruptures, changes, rearranges.

The directions led me to a different destination.
Nevertheless, I am here.

Write one word in
your journal every
day for one year.
Read the resulting
piece on New Year's
Eve at midnight.

Write everything you feel inside.
The more details the better.

KARMEN VASQUEZ, AGE 17

Admission

To a College Admissions Office:

If you knew you were like a genie in a lamp
would you grant me three wishes?
All I really need is two.
If you saw my grades and liked me, but saw my record,
would you change your mind and
judge me for words written in permanent ink?

If you knew my pains growing up, knew my struggles and troubles,
would you shun me and call me a burden to society
or take a chance on me and admit me to your college?

Everyday I wonder if I'm good enough –
How much sleep I've lost just thinking about it

You're my dream school.
Change my world and open doors for me.

Dogs bark at the door. It's the mailman.
Go to the mailbox.
Screams.

You Just Changed The Outcome Of My Future.
Thank you.

2

CHECKING MY MESSAGES EVERY FEW SECONDS

Technology

I went on a two-week backpacking trip in the canyons of Utah. When no one was making noise there was actually no noise. It led me to reflect that at no point in civilization had I ever experienced silence so completely.

Silence

Stop talking, they say.
Silence. It's the new thing.
It was invented just last year, along with the touchscreen Apple iPad.
It's free. You just have to stop talking. Amazing.

But it takes more than that.
Even they know somewhere in their subconscious that
Silence can't be found within fifty miles of a cellphone.

Ironic, that those who long most to find that elusive peaceful quiet
Will never in all their lives
Dare to go looking for it without their lifeline.
And they will never in all their lives
Truly find it
Until they do.

ANGELLE KING, AGE 15

This piece was inspired by a texting conversation I had with a friend who is always having boyfriend drama. I'm all for a nice relationship, but some of us need to stop taking it so seriously.

Heartbroken

She is heartbroken,
mind torn in two,
wondering,

Is this really true?

All of those promises
didn't
mean
a thing.

Or maybe they did?

Are you playing with her emotions
…again?!

I don't know why she becomes so
attached.

She's only 15.

Time and again, we all go through the same tough heartbreaks. This piece is based on various posts from my personal blog.

Blog of a Six-Month Heartache

March: *I hate you*
Something about how "it was always her, never you" hits me right in the gut because you are making it very clear that we never should have dated initially.

April: *Framed memories*
I look back at old photographs of us, and I don't think, "Wow, I wish I could go back to that time." I think, "Wow, I wish I was them." Two strangers' cheery grins stare back at me as if my mind won't bring back what my heart so fiercely tries to forget.

May: *Q & A*
Do you miss me? One day I'll either muster up the courage to ask or muster enough to move on.

June: *100%*
I know I'm not the first person you think to tell that hilarious story to or the first person you want to rant to, but when you do give me the chance to be that person, I'll always be here for you. I've never given you less than 100% of my attention. And if one day you realize that my 100% trumps the 99.99% that you get from her, then I'll still be here.

July: *And the anger fades*
I noticed today that I stopped checking my messages every few seconds for your text. I just stopped. It is pointless fighting for us, or you, for that matter. I'm tired of feeling second best. I'm closing the door. 3...2...1...Now.

August: *Change of heart*
We are reconnecting, but this time there is no lingering for a future, just hope for a friendship.

September: *Oh goodness*
...has it been six months already? No more wishing, sobbing, regretting. Time truly does heal those patches of pain. I can't even remember why I liked you. So long ole buddy crush.

So many things to blame not writing on. This particular day, I chose to pick on my laptop.

Case for Typewriters

I stroke a few keys, then hit the delete button with epileptic vigor.
I stare for what seems like an eternity,
then shut down Document 4 without naming it.
If it doesn't have a name,
it doesn't or didn't ever exist.
Which means, ultimately, that I didn't fail
at writing something.

DANIELLA FAURA, AGE 14

This piece was inspired by finding an old typewriter in my house.

Typewriter

on the very tips of my toes
I reach the shelf and see it
on top of a couple of thick dictionaries
next to the Atari console

the heavy machine made
clangs and cha-chings
the faded Orange Crush
a typewriter with Chiclet white keys

will this dinosaur work?
I blow off a blanket of dust
load some paper in
crack my knuckles and press

the first letter...nothing happens
I press again, still nothing
I unlock the machine
and try typing "Hello"

the machine awakens from its long slumber
my fingers tingle
dance around the keys
the music of letters stamping on paper

a writer's tool, waiting to share
tales of adventure

SAMANTHA JAMES, AGE 16

I wrote this poem in response to consumerism and the representation of humanity as a barcode.

Black and White

A code is what I am.

Refused among raw civilians,
withering, impatiently
and repeatedly in line.

The misconception.
The inner light;
Access denied.

No true pathway to freedom.
An imperishable contribution.
A cry that refuses compensation.

The guiltless consumer
and corrupted slither of distorted beeps.
The slicing after the bar code scans.

I am a code.
Concrete patterns,
black and white functions.
A code is what I am.

LYLA MATAR, AGE 16

The Song of the Modern Man

I hear a new invisible world singing –
the humming, chirping, whirring sound
of the modern man.

The rapid clicking of a text.
So much being said,
not a word uttered.
The syncopated beat of frantic typing,
procrastination taking its toll.
The anxious tapping of a pen
in a cubicle.
The warm words and face of a friend, miles away,
comforting us and making us lonely.
I know the secrecy an invisible world can give us,
and all the privacy it takes away.

The song of millions of things
we never had the courage to say ourselves,
millions of causes we pretend to support by clicking a button,
millions of dollars that we wish we had,
the song of a million hearts displaced by technology,
a million lies, threats, cheats, doubts and delusions
of falsely reasoned incognito states of mind, being and soul.

What happened to the song
that made us human?

Words exist for a reason, so why not use them?

This piece was written at a WriteGirl workshop where we listed all of our nicknames. It made me think of my first day of high school with a legendary teacher. She messed up my last name so much she resorted to calling me "Miss K."

Nicknames

I've always been used to the way people mess up my last name. It's Kownatzki, pronounced KUHV-NOT-SKI, in case you're wondering. Nothing, however, could have prepared me for the name I received on my first day of high school. My first class of the morning was with one of the oldest teachers in the school. Friends who'd had her before warned me that, although she is a great teacher for Algebra 2, she is also known for being a bit eccentric, to say it politely. So before I walked into her class, I took a deep breath and pulled on the door...to find it locked. Suddenly, a head with bright bug eyes popped out of the door.

"Oh, come in, take a card and stand at the back of the line along the wall," she said quickly. I grabbed the card and looked to my right at all the other students standing parallel to the wall. I slowly walked to the back of the line, looking at the different people. Their facial expressions varied from absolutely terrified to practically asleep. Almost everything in the room was related to math. There were posters on the wall, geometric dodecahedrons hanging from the ceiling. It was very intimidating. The bell rang sharply, waking everyone up.

"Okay, so I'll call out your name and you take a seat, okay? Oh wait..." She shuffled over to her cluttered desk. "Need my glasses," she said with a laugh. She put the glasses on with one hand, the roll sheet in the other, blinking as her eyes adjusted. She took a deep breath, calling out the names. I waited patiently, growing nervous as she read the J's.

"Miss...Kawasaki."

It was an interesting year.

This started out as a school assignment, but I changed it around to really make it my own.

I Am

I am the girl that writes what can't be said
pretends to be who she's not.

I wonder what life would be
if the things that happened…
didn't.

I hear the meanings of the words in music,
taste the pain and tears,
pretend to be the person I am not.
I feel loneliness and sadness inside,
touch the things I like,
worry about my family.

I wish I could someday be who I really am,
say what I think is right.
I dream of being the happiest person alive.
When no one is by my side, I shout inside my mind.

One day I will be set free,
declare that the world know I'm falling apart,
the pieces of a broken glass,
barely holding on.

This piece was inspired by a writing activity at the WriteGirl Creative Nonfiction Workshop at the Autry Museum.

My Name Is Danielle

My name doesn't define me; I define it. (Though it provides some creative direction.) Maybe I was predestined to write. My mom must've consulted the higher-ups while I was a fetus: "My daughter shall write!" Naming me after Ms. Steel just propelled her point, gave me an extra push in the right direction. Her wish was my command. I write, creating linguistic twirls of the tongue. My father added to my mixture with the creativity gene. He left shaping me to my mother, the master shape shifter.

My name carries all of my family. Each of my footprints and pen strokes embody someone in particular – my grandparents, father, uncles, brother, aunts and cousins, all mixed together becoming a smoothie that is Me. I am the combined effort of all those who've influenced me; they all left their mark.

My name is just a name for all of the things within me, merely the thing I respond to, and I'm using its connotation as a guide to the world.

This is about a place where I feel at home.

Still Home

Ocean tide
dried seaweed and distorted rocks
cover the land
clear blue sky, not a cloud in sight
hermit crabs fight over shells
I lie in the ocean
my arms and legs spread like a starfish
my breath held deep

I wish I was born here
in this water, this silent, beautiful water
so still
almost as though time is frozen
when it's not
I have to pay attention
through my goggles, past the air bubbles
to see the fish swimming by,
zooming along
to see the krill floating
I feel the current
a gentle push against me
making my hair float in all directions
calming like meditation
here, in this moment,
I feel free, here on Earth.

Take a deep
breath to calm
your pen. Write
as though you
are an exploding
supernova.

I actually said the opening line of this poem aloud.
I had just beaten my grandpa – my original teacher.

Ping Pong

My grandpa didn't teach me mercy; he taught me ping pong:
Long, slicing backhands that nearly graze the net
and tap the back of the table with a satisfying
"Plink!"
Serves with so much spin they bounce backwards.
And everything that goes into a serve like that –
Mischief
(the boy perched atop the drive-in wall, the dollar bill on the string,
stolen oranges, poison oak)
Determination
(the heart that refuses to quit, even when the pacemaker stops;
Organs that drink greedily from defibrillators
and burp with a flutter of life)
I come by mercy naturally. Take the crappie,
iridescent scales making rainbows in its underwater prison.
I am the girl whose tiny fingers tripped the wire door,
who watched its luminous body twist, hungry for protective depths,
happy not to eat something beautiful.
I come by mercy naturally. I might have let my grandpa,
an old man now with a shriveled hand, win.
Thank goodness he taught me ping pong.

I wrote this piece after my cousin was having a difficult time, and she leaned on me instead of the other way around.

Beautiful

Lounging like a cat on the wall,
her leg swinging like a tail,
her eyes tracking the sun.

I watch her,
scarlet flashes through swaying green.
She's vibrant,
wise,
beautiful,
fierce.

Lately, I am the one she leans on
as she casts long shadows of doubt.

Brown swirls around an oval face,
tracking the sun with her eyes.
Yearning for the setting sun,
the flame to smolder,
the day to end,
for thoughts to swirl out of her head
and follow the path of the wind.

The sun sets as the day ends.
She accepts
that she did the right thing.

I was at a WriteGirl Flash Workshop and one of the activities was to write about a simple object that had a deeper meaning. My mother's pearls were not real or fancy, which is perfect because my mother is simple and wonderful.

Mother's Pearls

She's getting ready –
Mousse in curls
Down to the last ringlet of hair –
Opens the worn out wooden drawer
Long pinched pink fingers
Shuffling in search

Gracefully faces me
Flattening out her hand
The lines of her palm are interrupted
by two white pieces of simplicity
Mommy crouches down and at my eye level
"Someday you will have your own pair of pearls"

Innocence in the air, I nod in agreement;
I want to be her
Real Pearls
Fake Pearls
My mother's pearls
She's who I aspire to be

This piece came from a writing activity about ancestors. I was reminded of all my family's secrets and how some have faded and some remain after so many generations.

Family Melody

Skeletons in the closet dance together.
Gaze into each other's eye sockets,
Hold each other's fleshless fingers.
> *Clank, clank*
> *Clank, clank*

Bones rattle.
Cha Cha to the tunes long unheard.
A rumbling rhumba of history.

Loud secrets and cold air
Between warm hearts
from long
ago.

Resurrect the spirit of the past with your words.

If you write
so much your
hands hurt,
you're on the
right track.

FAMILY

AMY HUYNH, AGE 18

An Ox's Tale

She sits in a protective position. Her narrowed eyes relax,
her worn body, so used to working hard, unwinds.
She begins in Teochew, our native tongue.
"What do you want to know?"
"Everything," I tell her.

Eighteen years old.
The Communists have taken over Vietnam, and her faith.
She hides away working at a factory –
she meets Father.

Twenty years old.
The boat is crowded, but freedom is worth the gold they paid.
Refuge in Indonesia is anything but easy.
The Americans give out food three times a week,
a year passes before they arrive in America.
Stepping off of the plane, her faith returns.

Sixty-two now, she gets up,
tells me she is hungry and commences making her lunch.
Sixteen years old, I look at her.
Time has made her strong.

Her will, determination and strength
course through my blood.

5
DANCE UNTIL THE MOON DIMS

Sleep & Dreams

I had severe insomnia for a while, and it became a large part of my life.

Insomnia

The average person falls asleep in seven minutes.
I think it's strange
A lot can happen
in seven
minutes.
Insomnia is worry, perpetual and illogical
and yet desperately justified
Time rushes through your veins
as all the tiny nuances of thought, perfectly normal in daylight
become trucks, trains
oppressively crushing, stifling.
Insomnia is wide eyes in the dark,
the strain of lying in bed.
The world becomes too much
as time melts   slowly   impossibly
Insomnia is waiting for sunrise,
for gaunt mornings and exhausted afternoons,
tense evenings and dark circles
and wondering what to do
while the rest of the universe slumbers.

LAUREN HEANEY, AGE 16

I wrote this at the season's first workshop after making a list of four objects that I feared. I chose one of them and wrote this poem.

Ticking Clocks

Rewind, reset, go
Never ending motions
Ringing alarms
Set to wake
Sleepless nights in subconscious thoughts
Ending the moments
When simply ignoring
A recurring sound becomes possible

Rewind, reset, go
Trap the daylight hours
Constrict all actions
Match the beating of a heart
Only to tick time down till the end

I am baffled by the fact that most people wait for specific circumstances or conditions in order to feel they are "allowed" to go after what they want.

Deferred Desire: Dream Pyre

i want to know
what the grasshoppers tell you as you lay your head against
the cool ground, losing your identity to the night

i want to know
what the stars say to you when your eyes plead with them,
begging for a wish that still hasn't come true

i want to know
what the clouds feel when you wake up in the morning and rub
hope out of your eyes, splash truth onto your face again and again,
until finally, you give up and find refuge back on the forest floor

i want to know
what crosses your mind as you sit and wait for moonlight to save you

 i want to know
 why you dream only after dark but hardly ever in the day

 but most of all:

 i want to know
 why sunlight isn't enough for your dreams to come true

ANNELIESE GELBERG, AGE 16

At a WriteGirl Editing Workshop, the activity was to write about a favorite place. I thought of my bedroom – but, more importantly, I thought of that place we all go when we're waking up or falling asleep.

Dreaming

Pillows caress my head as I snuggle deeper into the warmth of my stuffed animals. My eye opens just enough to see the blur of colors that is my wall – a collage of posters. I love it here – not just my bedroom, but here – this twilight place between rest and consciousness, with me smothered between purple covers. Desperate to return to a place of muddled dreams, I let my eyes drift closed… again… songs come sweetly to me and events that never happened linger in my mind. This is home.

This poem was pieced together from a train of thought I wrote one night in the early hours. My sleep-deprived imagination was fueled by the view outside my bedroom window.

Awake

In the black of the night I imagined times long past and people long dead
They stand beside my bed, too many ghosts in this dead world
Reminding me of the things I want to forget

There is too much sadness in this night city,
A city of dreams, with stars hidden by car smoke
Miles of rooftops, and the sound of a distant train

Out in a perfect world you can see the constellations
Hear the silence between the trees
when even the smallest creatures are asleep
But in the city the thunder of life keeps you awake
under the wide open sky

So many dreamers in the dark
How I shone in the dark

At the WriteGirl Poetry Workshop we were asked to think about our senses and to include details of touch, smell, taste in our poetry. Immediately what came to mind was my daughter's ability to predict rain by smell.

Because the air smelled of rain.

Raindrops, impatient suitor, beat on my bedroom window.
The green of clock radio glows 4:12 am.
I lie in bed, listen to the sound of thirsty leaves on the avocado tree.
I think of the parched Midwest where the cracked land
lolls out its tongue, begs for drops of water.
I tiptoe across cold floors on bare feet,
move from memory through a dark house
to the front door.
I stand beneath a black sky.
Drops drizzle down my face.
I recall a time long ago –
my daughter gazing skyward
arms raised
ready for the showers she knew would come
because the air smelled of rain.

I was three years old when I saw how the night becomes the dawn and the dawn becomes morning. Since then, I have been enamored with those hues of blue.

Dawn

5:30, 7:18
It's a shade of blue
yet not of cerulean.
It's a being –
a thinking,
realistic,
lively existence.

I sense Cobalt Emergence
when sneaking a glimpse of him.
(Yes, it is a he –
a boy who is so attractive
I never take my eyes off him.)

I just stare
at the window
watching my beloved
coming.
My heart sinks.

He left suddenly.
Dawn is afraid of Morning

Mornings

Mornings are the sirens blaring in your ears
BEEP BEEP BEEP
Cockadoodle doo, rise and shine
Up and at 'em, get out of bed, you lazy bum!

Mornings are the half-delusional "go away"
As the dream world fades from the
Crimson and the neon-Vegas-sign-yellow to the
Off-white of the ceiling and the washed out blue
Of those jeans you forgot to put away last night.

Mornings are those moments when the
First rays of sunshine tiptoe through
The cracks in your blinds, poking your eyes saying
"I'm awake. Everything's awake. There's a
World out there to explore."

Mornings are those times when you crack open your eyes
And you remember why it's called "mourning"
When you perform your sacred ritual, methodical and
Never changing, to commemorate the passing of a day
The end of an era, the disappearance of time.
When you realize that day-to-day existence you dreaded
Wasn't all that bad. Too bad it faded with the sunset.

Chronos

Ignore my ticking footsteps,
blind to your own shadow stretching
into the dusk.

Chaotic, un-tethered, I see you move
in your crooked lines,
out of step.

I am never tired or afraid of the dark.
I do not feel lonely, or dread the dawn.
But maybe at times I become

self-conscious.
Some Fridays at 4:59 pm,
when you fill my face with your watchful eyes,

and I hold your dreams and adventures
between my fingers.

You wait for me to blink.
You want me to change…

you stop resisting me.

Write at night. Your best ideas come after a full day of living.

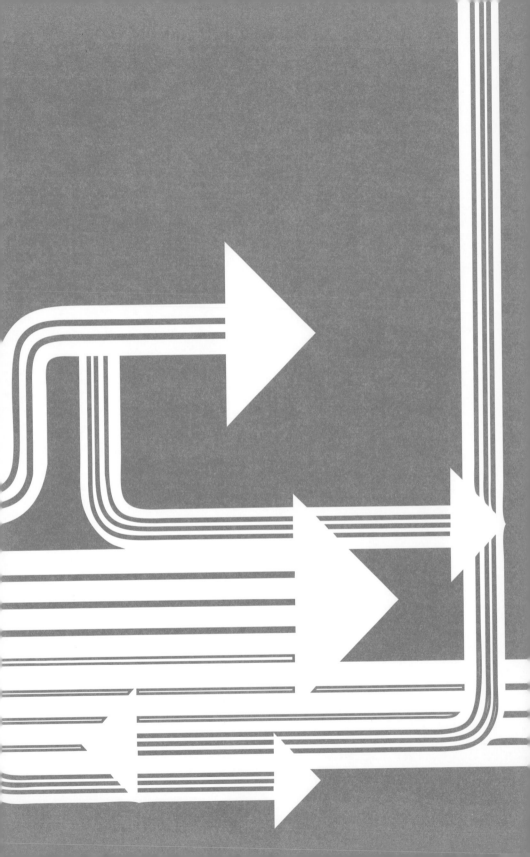

6

HER VOICE

Viewpoints

I wrote a response poem to Walt Whitman's "I Hear America Singing," just as Langston Hughes had with "I Too, America."

I, As Well

I, as well, sing, America
I sing with the choir, songs of freedom and tragedy.
Songs that were not born with me, but are a part of me.
Soft Filipino symphony; songs of the fifty stars and thirteen stripes

My generation only knows of the now
We sing the songs of pressure and the lack of knowledge, *they* all say
They chime and hum that we are the future, but *they* forget the lyrics and
Mutter under their breath, lose their faith.
My generation hears the broken record of discouragement;
feels the musical burden on repeat.

Tonight I'll put my headphones on and drown their out-of-place song.
Tomorrow we'll compose our own melodic future and lyrical plans.
My generation must praise them for putting us down, for we –

We will rise up and sing on their graves, songs of
how we made it and
how we made it better, together.

I, as well, sing, America.

JACQUELINE UY, AGE 15

A man told me I'd never be a journalist because there were few places for minorities in the news world. But reporters like Christiane Amanpour have taught me that he was wrong.

My Own

My tangled words, foreign and native,
Past and present.

Shaded eyes reveal his ignorance
at the color of my skin,
the culture in my eyes.

He said I couldn't make it
Clasping ideals of the past, outdated and useless
I search through the haze,
still weaving my way
trying to keep the peace
to find a way to be accepted.
But closed doors and chance stare at me
as I wait for the metro
that always seems to be late.

Night dissolves into early mornings
tired walking, days of headlines,
stories,
and newspapers.

Hoping for a better future
without thin walls and drifting voices.
I tell myself the day I shut the door
on my own face,
will be the day I've lost my own,
and my faith.

I wrote this because I know how people who are not originally from somewhere feel when they move to someplace new. I'm going through that right now, too.

We Are Leaders Too

Struggle for equality
To become an American Citizen
The family has great expectations
For you to study
To fight for your education
To be strong
Decisive
Show people that the saying
"You Do Not Belong" is not true.
Show people that we can be leaders too
No matter where we come from
Or what color we are.

The following poem was inspired by how much society impacts the self-esteem of individuals. It was written to all of the women who forget that they are beautiful.

The Things They Don't Tell You

They tell you your skin is beautiful,
But they don't tell you what shades are perfect.
Every size is beautiful,

But size 0 is perfect.
They tell you your face is beautiful,
But a pimple-less face is perfect.

Your figure is beautiful,
But they don't tell you a thin figure is perfect.
They tell you you're beautiful.

They don't see what beautiful really is.

For Our Own Sake

For our own sake
we haven't really
made progress
like an old scratched tape

Humans
should be respected
not abused
or neglected

This is not
an impediment –
it's the beginning
to a new environment

Women and men
are beautiful, valuable
should not be seen
as minimal

We are all
shining stars
no one has the right
to shut us down

KAYLYN GEORGE, AGE 17

I wrote this piece at a WriteGirl workshop. It was inspired by the feeling of always being put in a box and silenced just because I am a girl.

Does this dress fit?

Theft has been waiting, like the clock,
an ever-expanding man who thinks he owns the land,
stuck in his tower.

Mother has told me what to be
and what to do,
laced into a shoe and thrown in the gutter,
sinking while he thinks explorers are always alike
and everything is a copy of the copy.

One will be accused.
One will not have a name.

The Judge was conniving and sentenced
to the flowers, while brains and milk have gone sour
by the minute.

Is it a disgrace
that they wasted intelligence on your name?
The little girl dances idle, sentenced for her dress.

Sentenced for her voice
waiting to write. Sifting for freedom,
ready to mend her dress
outside the man's pocket.

Create like an
architect creates
buildings — start
with a blueprint.

EMILY BURTON, AGE 15

One of my favorite quotes is something a character said on TV. When asked if he supported the war, he said, "I support the men fighting it." It's important to remember how much families lose when a hero dies.

Ty's River

"Beautiful, isn't it? Like the water's dancing."
I stare down at the churning river remembering his voice that is more beautiful than anything, even his precious Mississippi, and with a Southern drawl thicker than honey.

"Because fighting to keep your head above water is so much fun."
I never understood his love for the river, with its crashing white rapids and sharp, slick rocks. Then again, I never understood a lot about him.

"You shouldn't be so scared of everything, Rach. You'll miss out."
I slip out of my ballet flats, determination flowing through me.

"I'm not swimming in that deathtrap, Ty."
I squeeze my eyes shut and dip one toe into the icy water.

"Well I am. There aren't exactly going to be swimming pools in Iraq. Come in with me."
The river swirls around my waist. I shiver.

"Not in your lifetime!"
I dive in and float on the rippling water, staring up at the summer sky.

"I guess sometimes a guy's just gotta go things alone."
With my eyes closed, I pretend my brother is floating next to me.

I wish you were here, Ty.

7

SCORCHED BUT LEGIBLE

Other Worlds

It's okay to
write something
that doesn't
make sense.

"See ya soon, Dollface."

Marie was left alone, pounding desperately at his grave, draping his tombstone in painful tears for the love lost with his spirit. She never even got the chance to tell him those three big, *crucial* words.

Someone tapped her on the shoulder, and that jerked her back to reality. "What?" she growled.

Marie spun around to meet dazzling sapphires and a striking, cocky grin. "Hey, Dollface."

"Daniel?"

This story started out as a dream. When I woke up, I wrote down as much of it as I could. Here is a section of it.

Ren

I knocked heavily on Will's door. "It's over, Will." I managed to sound cross while not falling asleep, a miracle in itself. "God, just let me in, all right?"

The door swung open, and, as Will swept me up in a hug, I practically fell asleep there in his arms. "Just stay awake for a little longer, Ren," he said. "Where's the bullet wound?"

His voice penetrated my fog of pain, and I indicated with my head that it was my right shoulder. At that moment blinding pain turned my vision white, and a scream ripped from my throat. My eyes rolled to the back of my head, and I collapsed.

I woke up to an unfamiliar warmth on my arm that somehow felt like… sunlight. I smiled, opening my eyes. Will was at my side in an instant. My arm was rebandaged with crisp white linens. I guess he had changed them while I was unconscious.

"Are you okay?" he asked. There were shadows under his eyes and his hair was messed up, as if he hadn't slept in days.

"Yeah," I rasped, "How long was I…asleep?" Will sighed as he hesitated, running a hand through his dark hair. "Five days."

"What?" I asked warily.

"He came to see you. I tried to stop him, but he came in anyway. He was laughing and –" Will shuddered. "He said things were going as planned."

I felt nauseous, but I had to ask, "The stuff in the syringe. What do you think it was?"

Will shrugged, "We'll find out soon enough."

AMY MCGRANAHAN, MENTOR

Written after a discussion about the wild world of ballet with my mentee, Zoe, during the WriteGirl Memoir Workshop.

To Mowgli

Chance festooned the saloon, damp with heaving history. In quiver and covey and bevy and troop, we migrated from the curmudgeonly stage to the only lighted windows for hundreds of miles. Crowded in this old room, smelling of generations of costume and debauchery, a man asked my best friend if she could play it again. Marching her fingers over creamy keys, he gave her a dollar to play his favorite song: Chopsticks. The town joined us, finally, in awkward dancing of every ilk. None of the townspeople minded, though. Proud and cheerful, giddy steps unabashed, they looked at peace with something our nervous ballet menagerie hadn't figured out.

LAUREN DAVILA, AGE 17

I wrote this piece during a WriteGirl Fiction Workshop.
It was inspired by a red masquerade mask.

Waltz of Propriety

The music of the waltz through the ballroom was cut off as the doors behind me closed. In my red mask, I was just another girl, at another ball, with no titles, no expectations. My gown rustled as I turned into a hallway that stretched on forever. I held the red rose tied with a black ribbon he had given me. Letting it drop, I walked on. I passed a girl, her eyelashes fluttering as fast as the fan she held. She laughed coyly at what her companion said, and I crossed the hall, leaving them alone in their young love. I stopped at an open window and watched the raindrops fall on the moors outside. I could smell the rain, freedom, something I didn't have.

I stayed a while and then walked back towards the ballroom, fighting the train of my dress that tried to keep me at the window, but I pushed past it, my sense of propriety overwhelming my desire for freedom. I passed the spot where the couple had stood and saw the girl, fan discarded on the ground, once fluttering eyelashes covered in tears, sobs filling the silence of rejected love. My rose lay on the ground, brown and withered, ribbon trampled and frayed. I stepped over it, and at the door, I removed my mask, hesitantly putting on the tiara that lay there.

I wrote this around December 21, 2012, when the world was supposed to end. When it didn't, I laughed and began thinking about the future, when the world will inevitably end.

The Imponderable Day the World Ends

Just as the sun goes out, your laptop shuts down for the first time in months. The battery finally died, and you lost the charger somewhere behind the couch – the same place you lost the last Twinkie and your Chihuahua, Ricky. Now your digital reality has ended, and you're waking up to a sunless nightmare.

I, on the other hand, am sitting on the edge of Perkin's Pier, two miles from your house. Unlike the rest of the world, I knew that the sun was dying. Horatio had been sending me scorched but legible letters over the past decade, about how he was feeling a bit tired after billions of years burning. The last one read, "It's time for retirement. Say goodbye to Marceline for me. Tell her I love her."

Eight minutes later, he was out, as if the great Creator blew out his flame. Now, there is nothing but the glow of luminous waste on the surface of the water, and blue-white illumination coming from the windows on Mariposa Avenue. I fold the parchment into a crane, and pin it to the shoulder of my faded denim jacket. I will miss that sun.

I find the Lisa Narwhal floating solitarily in the incandescent water and set sail for Marceline, the moon. After what feels like a full day of sailing, I reach her. She seems melancholy; I don't blame her. I would be, too, if my husband went out as suddenly as Horatio did. I find the ladder stored in the hull of my boat, unroll it, and climb up to her. I show her Horatio's letter. She smiles a bit, followed by a flood of silvery tears. I decide to stay with her and to become her companion until the end.

Writing is an expansion of the known and unknown world.

8

THE WAY SHE SPOKE

Portraits

Her Words Were the First Storm

Her words were cool wind that escaped her mouth.
Like rain before a thunderstorm,
it seemed like she was worried about something –
the way she spoke
she was a glass close to shattering.

Her words were dreary rain that danced on your window pane.
She was a solemn song
sinking slowly,
steadily, leisurely.

Her words were ice,
sickles of frozen water from the cave that created them.
Eyes cold as winter, she spoke,
frozen,
isolated,
a glacier slowly melting in the middle of the Arctic.

Her words were a flood,
they trickled out of her mouth hastily.
Her body shook like an earthquake,
her head swirled like a tornado with the power of a thousand cities.
This was the first storm.

I wrote this piece as I was waiting for a friend at a park near my house. Sitting next to me was a middle-aged man observing a massive train of ants moving through a crevice in the concrete.

Ants

He had watched ants travel
Single file
Down a crack in the concrete
Their tiny bodies pushing,
Beyond intertwined
Seeming to him a long black trail
And he prayed to God to be one of them
One mind with one goal
Belonging to something bigger than himself
Living in chaos
But living in order

I wrote this when I was in an especially good mood, and when I was also really craving chocolate. It explores the idea of innocence, living with a strict parent and a child trying to understand how the world works.

The Mission

Block one: The trees sped by as Jeremy ran, backpack securely around his shoulders, a fortune cookie carefully clutched in his hand. It was crucial that the cookie stay intact. Home was an entire six blocks away, but Megan was hopefully still distracting Father with long-answer-provoking questions. The two of them had spent the week prior to the mission doing nothing but laborious preparation. It had been the longest week of Jeremy's life. *It's funny how time can slow down and speed up without really changing at all*, he thought, gaining speed. He hoped that time would choose this moment to slow down.

Block two: There was a dog that lived in the corner house on this street, so Jeremy made sure to cross to the other side. Megan had been in charge of scoping out the neighborhood for him. She even asked Father to take her to the new smoothie place. Father had agreed but only to show Megan how much sugar was in the average smoothie. Megan had seemed fine when she got home, but later, when everyone was asleep, she woke up her brother as she often did when something was wrong.

"Jer, I don't understand," she had said that night, sitting on the edge of his bed.

"It's okay Megs, Father just has his ways."

"But his ways aren't like anybody else's."

"You don't know that," Jeremy told her soothingly.

"He'll be furious if he catches us," Megan said.

"That's the fun of it," Jeremy replied. "There's no need to cry, Megan."

Later, after Megan had gone back to sleep, Jeremy lay awake worrying about his sister with a parent-like ache. The mission was dangerous, but necessary for both of them.

Trust Issues

He trusts no one
for fear of being hurt.
There is a threat
around every corner,
behind every door.
and he knows it.

No one gets close,
they don't even try anymore.
He pushes away anyone who cares.

He trusts no one,
not his family,
not his pets,
not even himself.

He fears being left.
He chains up his heart.

No trust.
No love.
No honesty.
He's alone in this wide world, crowded with people.
And he likes it that way.

This was inspired by an assignment in my creative writing class.

That Girl

She walked with a certain confidence.
It couldn't be easily ignored.
Always impeccably put together,
never a hair out of place,
eyebrows plucked to perfection.

She came to school in a fancy black car,
never looked at anybody.
I got jealous,
longing for the day when she looked at me,
invited me to one of her parties,
in with the cool crowd.
But jealousy isn't real.

I wonder if she liked all the pool parties, the attention?
What did she really feel
behind those lively green eyes
and the masked words?
Maybe inside she is breaking apart at the seams.

SHARMIN SHANUR, AGE 14

I wrote this poem while thinking about a little girl oblivious to the world and grasping at her innocence.

Blue Sky and Blooming Stars

I sat in the midst of it all
Taking in the smell of the blooming stars
I remember looking up into the blue sky and then...
I couldn't breathe

The blue sky turned black and all I saw were my little hands
I stared at them for days
The winter's bone held me tight
My eyes saw the cracks of life
I lay there under blue sky and blooming stars

Song of Grief

Child
hurt, cracked, broken, furious
cheeks and ears hot as fire
hands and lips tremble faster, stronger
than a 10.5 earthquake
Eyes look up, keep the tide from
overflowing
pupils make sense of blurry-smooth flying
water particles, ready to dance

A show with loud drums
an incredible light show
only Nature knows how to create
Down come dancers, leaping
on stage with dramatic effect, mimicking
what consumes her heart

Moving with the music that is thunder
child moves on to the stage
dancers cross her body like brush on canvas
child smiles
the sky has done its job, a creature
so wide and mysterious decided
to cry so this child could
laugh and dance
to the song that used to be her grief

Don't be afraid
of where your
inspiration stems
from. It doesn't
matter if it's
from a dream,
while taking a
test, or even in
the shower –
let it take you
where it wants
to go.

KRISTA GELEV, AGE 16

I love thinking about the history of a room, the innumerable stories embedded in its furniture and walls.

Sacred Space

She waltzes alone in an empty room
To records only she can hear
Stopping once in a while
To readjust the needle on an ancient gramophone

When she grows hungry she ambles into the next room
An opera diva in a silk robe, an artist's muse, a queen of no nation
Her only sustenance the feasts she's read about
In dusty leather volumes
Atop tall shelves
Inhaling yellowed pages
Kissing marbled covers

Her pink hands caress
The creaky wooden banister
Her assured feet tread on threadbare rugs
Only she is sensitive to what's long been forgotten

This room has seen thousands of nightfalls,
The tender gradations of billion-year-old light
To watch the walls go from gold to violet for an evening
Is to absorb the fullness of decades

9

LET ME USE YOUR USE YOUR CHAPSTICK

Love

This falls under the theme "Cautionary Tales for the Young and Recklessly in Love" and is about the difficulties of juvenile infatuation, so others will know they're not alone!

I Wanted to Tell You that I Loved You

I wanted to tell you that I loved you
So you would let me use your Chapstick
So we could plant a turnip garden
And fight in the Trader Joe's parking lot
I wanted to tell you that I loved you
So that we could say things are stupid
But do them anyway
And eat Chinese food in my bed
And we would never be lonely
After watching Annie Hall
I wanted to tell you that I loved you
So we could live south of the boulevard
In a multi-million dollar house
But only stay in one room
Because we don't need so much space

But if I had told you that I loved you
You might have kissed me all the way down to my knee caps
And then taken the next plane to New York
And called me to say you weren't coming back
I couldn't tell you that I loved you
Because my fingers were in my mouth
I cried in Annie Hall and never planted a turnip garden
I had to buy some Burt's Bees
But I never used it
So my lips got swollen and cracked
And my throat got too dry
So I could never tell you that I loved you

KATE JOHANNESEN, AGE 18

I initially wrote this as a private journal entry, but then realized it would be good to share because I felt a lot of other girls would be able to relate.

Want the Unwanted

I want the unwanted boys
The loners, the outcasts,
The mismatched socks.
Give me your gingers,
Your nerds,
Your weird art kids,
Your intellectuals!
Bring me your friendless,
Your tall and skinny-boned huddled masses!
Send them to me,
And I will make them mine.

I will offer up my person for cuddling;
My brain for thinking, wishing, dreaming, learning and understanding;
My ears for listening;
My mouth for kissing, talking and reading aloud;
My hands for holding;
My heart for stealing and never returning.

They say one man's trash is another man's treasure.
I say the guy that gives other girls a rash is my guilty pleasure.

I've been writing lots of short stories this year. This one is about someone who is unusually sensitive to love.

Unattached

The first time he kissed me, my ear fell off. Nothing like that had ever happened to me before. I don't know what caused it, but I'm guessing that being near him got me so excited that my cells forgot to stick together.

When my ear fell to the ground, he said, "Are you okay?" And I said yes, because I was. There was no blood, no pain. The ear just wasn't part of me anymore. That's how it went. I kept losing pieces. He didn't mind. He'd been clear from the start that he was attracted to what was on the inside.

Soon, each of my cells separated. There was none of me left to hold or to hug, and I could tell he missed me. After a few days, though, he started to sense my energy. He reached out to caress it, and the infinitesimal pieces of me broke up even smaller.

When I was with him, near him, around him, my body just kind of let go. If someone had warned me about it ahead of time, I probably would've said, never mind then, I won't kiss him. But there was no warning, and I was caught up in it before I realized what was happening.

Soon I was so small that he could breathe me in, and he did. Oh! The feeling of being surrounded by love and lungs! So warm, so cushy, so safe.

Don't. Don't for one second think of me as self-destructive, as lost. If that's how it sounds, you've got it all wrong.

I'm just different, on a molecular level. This thing with him has turned me into something better than human. I'm part of the universe now. I can be anything I want.

Sightlessly in Love

I was forcing myself
against him.
Did I not realize
he didn't want me?
Did my love for him
make me blind?
He picked her
over me.
He couldn't even
look me in the eye
when their relationship
fell apart.
I was still in love,
sightlessly in love.

I wrote this about a boy I admired. I liked him and I'm pretty sure he liked me.

Speak the Unspoken

I see you.
You see me.
We see us, but you don't speak.

"Is it too early?" I question myself.
"Definitely not," I tell myself.

I see you.
So then I speak.
You speak back, your words are weak.

Why oh why is speaking so hard?
Well maybe it's me just trying too hard.
"Trying too hard?" I question my motives.
Motives, motives, I question my motives.

"Is it too early?" I question myself.
"Definitely not," I tell myself.

Today I saw you.
You saw me.
We see each other, but no one speaks.

When you are writing,
let it flow out. You can
always revise later.

I wrote this poem at the editing workshop. I want young girls to understand that the boy they gush over may look good from afar, but might not be the best catch, up-close and personal.

Secret Admirer

I'll admire you from a distance
fearing the up close and personal

trapped by your pearly white teeth
seeing the darkness in your eyes

I would hate to sink in quicksand
longing, making me believe

I would hate for you to play bandit
stealing my heart and my dreams

good boy from afar
I hear the angels sing

devil in disguise
I watch the skies darken

my insides begin to burn
I protect my wounds

conceal my vulnerability
and admire you from a distance

I write poems in business meetings. Don't tell anyone.

Wednesday Meeting

With eyes and fingers
Intent on his laptop he
Thinks about numbers and lunches and reports
While he listens to the meeting
Speaking up when he has something to contribute
He crosses off the calls he made from the car
Multi-tasking the same way I
Listen to audiobooks while I type up the minutes
Except
He's not sitting there thinking about kissing me.

I wrote this for a friend. I was inspired by some of her experiences with a certain awkwardly beautiful guy.

Innocent Encounters

There is innocence in the awkward
perfection in her feelings.
But let's hope against hope that maybe
(just maybe!)
his feelings –
they may be mutual.

The barely-there touches,
secret glances.
their conversations,
sounds of a future and a relationship
that can and may just
amplify what has yet to be
ruined.

And even after that,
the ink is not yet dry.
But when it happens –
when the ink dries,
and the smoke clears,
and all is said and done –
it will be epic.

Blue

Turquoise, aqua, cobalt,
but really just blue.
The clear morning sky,
with sparrows in the air, learning to fly.
Speckled dazzling gems
on my white dress, adorned at the hems.

Gleams from one special thing,
the colored stone on my tiny wedding ring.
The deep calm sea,
where we will eventually explore – just you and me.
All these shades through and through,
represent the times with just me and you.

Betrayal

You lie
You run
You never come back
You betray
Can I trust you?
I don't know anymore
Who you are
What you want
Why you are here
Who, what, where, why
Why would you do this to me
I thought you loved me
I thought you cared for me
You say, "I never want to see you hurt"
But look at what you did to me

We said vows
That we would never betray
Yet you went behind my back
After I poured myself
You just ran
Left
Went away
With no goodbye
No explanation
You just left
And left me
With my broken bones
Here to stay.

CHELSEY MONROE, MENTOR

This came from a writing experiment I did with my mentee where we had to integrate seven random words into our poetry.

Making Returns

Please return our love.
The receipt is in my left pocket.
I believe the model is broken –
it never worked quite right.

After reading very sad fiction that left a cliffhanger at the end, I decided to write something in that style.

The Red Camellia

She grunts as she hauls her heavy, dark blue workbag with dirt all over it up the never-ending stairs to the apartment too small to be called home. She flings her bag onto the table and collapses like a lifeless rag doll onto the pile of clothes she calls a sofa. For some bizarre reason, she has always found the pile comforting and welcoming. It contains her shirt with holes all over it like decorations on a Christmas tree, a t-shirt smelling like party balloons and jeans she keeps as a memory. But ever since he disappeared…

She tilts her head so she can see the calendar with its torn corners. A dried up, unusually red camellia lies peacefully next to it. She is terrified of the camellia, too horrified to even touch it because whenever she gazes at it, the camellia drains energy out of her like a nightmare haunting her day.

Looking at the flower, her breathing quickens as a scent washes over her, covering her up like a blanket, wrapping her in its bubble, and engulfing her in its embrace. It is a scent so painfully familiar that she recognizes it immediately. His scent.

MELANIE ZOEY WEINSTEIN, MENTOR

When sick, expect to have symptoms until the heart is fully healed.

Heart Break, the Illness

You can go to the movies,
laugh at a diner, fold your clothes,
work out, stay out,
redirect conversations,
get a haircut,
buy organic toothpaste,
eat Whole Foods sushi,
drink Emergen-C,
look your best, seem your best –

Sudden moments of paralysis.
Tears that leak in your sleep,
drip-drops from the shower head
hours after the water's been turned off.

Some road trips are terrible; those following breakups especially so. I wrote this at the Creative Nonfiction Workshop at the Autry.

Santa Cruz Blues

A sudden hairpin turn snapped me against the suitcases. One of my headphones fell out, and the bassline was flooded with beardy, overalled twang. With the self-conscious despair of fourteenhood I stuffed it back into my ear and debated, softly sobbing to complete the effect – deciding instead that what People in my Situation do is write. I don't remember whether I slunk low against the seatback and made a pageant of myself, but I set myself to the furious scribbling peculiar to heartbreak.

My songs were tuneless, like the old man outside the coffee shop warbling "The First Noel" into the dusk, but they cut like safety pins through butter and *hurt* – like dying stars, cigarette burns, whiskey burns, dark like the crackle of charcoal from where your hair touched me, like the secrets you carried under your bracelets –

You broke me, love, my world shattered around your absence – and I am crammed into a Highlander and you, in your tragic immolated confusion – you have no idea.

The road straightened, the song ended, and with it the wiry tightness across my shoulders. I debated, self-consciously, slowly, what it might be like to move on.

Let your pen do the talking.
Allow your imagination to
engulf you!

10

LIQUID LITERATURE

Write & Read

I literally wrote this on the night before the deadline (shh... I wasn't supposed to tell you that). This is more or less what happened.

Jolt of Lightning

I don't know what to write. I'm serious – I really don't know what to write. It's late at night, the deadline is tomorrow, and my inspiration level is close to nonexistent. This is what my writing looks like so far:

Nothing. It's a Very Blank Page.

I have no idea what to write. I look up some inspiring quotes. I flip through a couple of my old middle school notebooks, tap a pencil against the desk. I sigh. I wonder what I'm going to write about. I try writing a poem about shadows, but the idea of "fleeting dancers flickering" doesn't sound quite right. I skim through old magazines, but for some reason, the national debt and the 2013 Oscar predictions don't seem to go along together in a story.

Still no inspiration.

I trace little designs with my finger in the dust gathering on the bookshelf next to me. I eat a banana out of boredom. After twenty more minutes, this is what my paper looks like:

Still nothing. None. Zero. Blank Page.

I stare up at the ceiling, trying to match up all of the tiny cracks like constellations. I watch the minutes slowly crawl by on the clock, the minute hand inching ever so slowly. 8:45. 8:50. 9:00. Sometime between watching the clock strike 9:15 and looking around the room for random inspiration, Inspiration suddenly hits me. It feels like a shock to my system. A breath of crisp air. An exhilarating jolt of lightning. I have Inspiration! Inspiration is mine!

I decide to write about trying to write – about trying to figure out what I'm going to write. I write about right now, about unblocking my writer's block. I'm here, and it's now. I'm writing about *write* here and *write now*.

This is my foolproof way to get inspiration when I'm stuck.

Tap In

I sit down, blank screen, cursor mocking.
Nothing comes. I lose hope.
My negative ego mobilizes dark forces.
Get up. Drink coffee. Eat something.
Not productive avoidance…physical fortification.
I sit down again, eyes closed, waiting. Listening.
Behold, the muse arrives.
Tap in. Trust.
She is always there.
Waiting for you to call her.

I was asked to explain how someone comes to identify him or herself as a writer, and to define what it really means to be a writer.

If I Were a Writer

I'm not a writer,
but if I were:

I would line up stories on city streets, pour liquid literature into
fountains, and assure the stars that they exist only for the sake of simile

I would strangle reality with metaphors, stitch paradoxes
into daily life, and personify words just so I could take them
out for coffee and get to know them all one-on-one

I would trap my readers in stanzas and let them ricochet
between couplets, while they argue endlessly that their lives
are somehow mirrored in my prose

I'm not a writer,
but if I were:

I would write until I could convince the universe to
swallow its secrets and spit back poetry

ZHITONG QIU, AGE 17

I love the color of words that bring out so many different emotions.

Words

Sprinkled high with meanings,
floating around the pages,
creating colorful sentences

to be tasted by the lips,
As the mouth sounds out the syllables.

The aroma of the sweet and sour phrases
that fills the once blank page.

Bittersweet emotions scattered in every word,
wonder flows through each paragraph.

It's enchanting, beautiful,
these words shaped by feelings,
created to make something delicious.

I began this poem with the girls. Sometimes it's hard to write when someone else is asking you to do it. It's also good to write this way – eventually you will be moved to write. "Tell me to write!" you might not even know you are thinking.

Language

If I couldn't tell you my stories
then the lake of my mind would dry up for sure
my tongue sad, forlorn in a mouth without words
thought flat without tone or timbre to it
And if I couldn't write about myself
then I couldn't get to that deeper layer of meaning
that makes all of life matter
Let me write you something now then
while I still have the chance
about the lake of the first language
to do so, I need to go back
  to language, I mean
        the first, that is
likely the result of a genetic mutation
in an early group of Homo sapiens
living 150,000 years ago on the banks of a large body of
fresh water in Central Africa
      this language nuanced, changed in increments of
twenty miles or so as settlements grew separate from
that original one
  and life without language? I don't care for it
give me language, the first, the second, the last
the lake is still in me somewhere
I walk its edges at times
or plunge to its depths and
I have by now identified within me a longing
If I couldn't tell you these things about myself
then I don't think I could be a poet.

My Notebook

My notebook, well, I really don't use it much. It stays in my backpack, most of the time. It's neither too big nor too small. It's a dark pink color. It reminds me of how I used to think I had no heart or humor. I carry it around so my backpack won't feel so lonely. I carry it around because it makes my backpack look a little bit more heavy. I use my notebook to look smart, but most people don't know that, so let's keep it a secret!

In middle school, I used my writing as a way to get through the struggles of being shy.

Making Friends

I am sprinting now. With each footstep reality becomes nothing more than a blur of colors and a jumble of meaningless sounds. Buildings and people blend together, their voices disappear. The taunting, the teasing, the laughter, the name calling, it all disappears!

My running slows, and I begin to walk, taking notice of my new surroundings. In place of the people, creatures odd and wonderful. In place of the buildings, enormous moss-covered trees that reach up tangling their branches in the clouds. In place of the pavement, wet black soil, sprouting with toadstools that glow under the stars. In place of the voices, the clicks and chirps of animals only found in the wildest of my fantasies. I am free. Finally I am free! I twirl around in my new world, the one woven from whispers and stitched up by dreams, the one I created from a blank sheet of paper, now filled with the words that spin around in my head, dancing and twirling along with me.

When I stop twirling I am dizzy and one of the creatures catches me as I tumble to the forest floor. I stare up at him, into his big golden eyes and I know that in this moment, in this world, I will never be alone.

My name is Charlie, and I *do* have friends, I know because I made them myself, with a sheet of paper and a pen.

ELIZABETH WANER, AGE 16

I constantly find myself struggling with choosing the exact word to express exactly what I feel.

Poetry

It seems almost impossible.
To transition a thought from one's brain to paper.
To evoke that exact feeling in words.

It is a difficult task to depict
every
detail
in a concrete way.

To express myself,
without changing the expression.

Many poets manage to do it.
They manage to express exactly what they feel
in a few words.
They depict an emotion
through lyrics and beats.

So, why have I,
who enjoy this so thoroughly,
not managed to define
that one feeling?

Creation

Grabbing hold of an ink spell
An eruption of pure power
To weave a theoretical rainbow
A story of untold mystics

I dream you inside out
Finding you in history's hipbone
Fractal myths flowing into a mass of ink
Until your story is complete

STEPHANIE NICHOLS, AGE 14

This poem is about an everyday item that means so much to me: my pen. Doesn't matter if it's black or blue, click-y or non.

Click Clack

I sat in our spot
Clicking my pen
Click clack
Click clack
Yes, I was here
But just wait
A thought entered my mind
Quickly, I wrote
No longer with others
Now a superhero
I ran across rooftops
Heels clicking
Click clack
Click clack
I look up from my paper
Thinking, once again here
I sat in our spot
Clicking my pen

When I was just learning to read, I searched for myself in the stories I read. I remember how I felt when I thought I'd finally found one.

In Search of the Imperfect Girl

From the minute I could read, I dove right in. I plowed through stacks of books about dogs and bears and families of potato heads. In tamer stories, little girls pushed dolls in strollers while small dogs nipped at their unscuffed heels. Their golden curls were held in place with flawless bows. These stories about girls named Sally and Jane were never my favorites, but I read them anyway, as a detached observer, mildly intrigued by the ways of others.

I had no interest in dolls unless they could fly. Barbies were launched as makeshift planes, landing on a bedroom floor covered in Hot Wheels tracks. I chafed at the thought of tights, sobbed when my mom combed through my tangles, pouted as she pasted sticky curls around my face with gooey, pink Dippity Do.

One day, I found a story about a girl who wore overalls and jeans. Raised by a widowed father who didn't know much about girls, she spent blissful days digging for earthworms and climbing trees. Her knees were skinned, her hair was a mess. I flipped each page, excited to see what she'd do next: climb a mountain, sail the world, artfully dodge hot rollers and their evil, sharp white spikes? But she didn't. Somewhere in between the tree climbing and grub catching, her father remarried.

Within a few short pages, she was introduced to all the joys of approved girlhood, and to my horror, she liked it. I squirmed as she embraced a new doll, gasped as she happily donned a frilly dress, screamed, "Nooo!" as she gleefully burned her jeans and overalls in a giant bonfire.

I read with one eye open as the sparkling new girl thanked her stepmother for showing her the way to true happiness, then dropped the book among the Barbies and opened another.

Road signs and billboards can be inspiration.

Past and present –
mix it all together
to make a story.

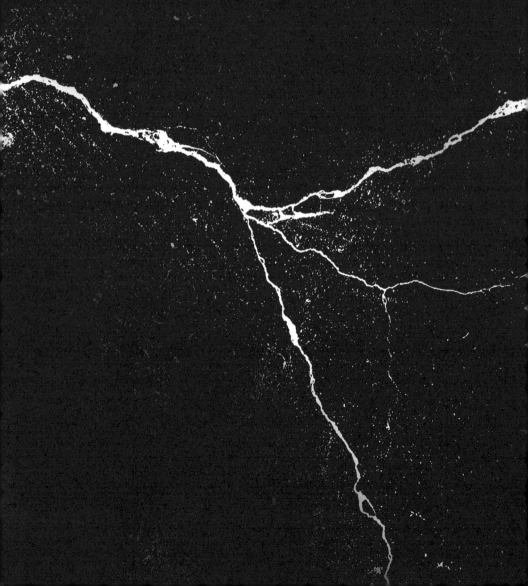

CASSIE SHIMA, AGE 16

After I finished reading The Night Circus by Erin Morgenstern, I felt so abandoned and lonely. I began thinking about that feeling, so, I wrote this.

The end.

It comes at the end of every good book:
the end.
The world you thought you were a part of,
the world that seemed so much better than
your own, disappears
with the flip
of a page.
Before long, you come to the bitter realization that
you were nothing
but a curious spectator,
playing word-turned films
inside your head.

11

SING IT TO YOURSELF

Music

HEATHER LIM, AGE 14

This piece is about my daily routine in the morning as I wait at the bus stop. Music makes the world look different to me.

Bus Tunes

She walks out into the cold morning atmosphere,
Huffing out clouds of hot breath into the Californian air.
While waiting at the bus stop,
She jams her favorite tune of the moment into her ears,
Hoping the crankiness will fade.
Hair is sticking out in every direction,
But she doesn't really care.
As she slightly bobs her head to the music,
She gets lost in her own world.

*I wrote "Neverland" at the WriteGirl Poetry Workshop
and decided to make it into a song. It sounds really
cutesy and fun.*

Neverland

You can wear that
sailor hat I bought you,
down by the Queen Mary.
the wind is blowin' strong, we hold fast.

Take me on your way to Neverland
flyin' over town and in hand
detach your shadows
my Peter Pan

With ribbons in my hair,
love is in the air
Tell me that you won't stray,
let's just sway
drink Orange Crush
and run away

Take me on your way to Neverland
flyin' over town and in hand
detach your shadows
and let's fly, fly, fly.

I had a crush on this guy. He played a song for me on his iPod, and this came from it.

There's Always One Song

One line, one word, one melody that reminds you of them
Reminds you of the times you two shared
The laughs you've had
The secrets you've told
And the long night conversations
That never seem to end
The song plays through your head constantly
Reminding you of the first time you heard it
You spent the day figuring out what song it was
You know every word
Every line
Every verse
Every melody
Every part of it
So at night when the song isn't playing
You can sing it to yourself and remember

I wrote this after hearing the word "heartstring" in several different songs.

An Undefined Cymbal

these days
these old strings on my heart
feel so out of tune

I play them endlessly
but all that comes out
is a distressed cacophony

and playing them, so dissonant,
seems to come through
as a badly rehearsed elegy

it lacerates the ears
it grates and claws and wails
Schrodinger's Cat just wants to prove he's still alive

so I take refuge in
this hollow-bodied instrument
I call a home

AMAYA MCGINNIS, AGE 17

This song is a celebration that a relationship was ending.

Didn't I?

Verse
We've had some good years
This goodbye doesn't call for tears
Wish me luck
Give me a kiss
I know there won't be much about me
that you'll miss

Pre-chorus
But maybe when you've got some time
You'll leave her side and rewind
To the time you got the flu
And I took care of you
When your mother died
And when I held your hand while you cried
And when we planned to run away
Make a good life for ourselves one day

Chorus
So please don't forget me completely
I loved you so sweetly
Didn't I?
I doubt we'll remember this always
But maybe on Sundays
You'll think and sigh

RACHAEL WANG, AGE 13

This song was inspired by an event at my school
called IMPACT. It's about popularity and how you
have to act to stay in, instead of out.

One of Us

Chorus:
You can't be one of us if you aren't mean
You can't be one of us if you aren't seen
You can't be one of us if you think or cry
You can't be one of us if you don't believe
We are the only ones that can survive

As you walk out the house
You turn into a mouse
Get in a group or get out
Enter a tribe or get trampled
If you aren't one of us
You're a loner and a loser

Chorus

In the courtyard, where things get wild
Before you get hit, join a pile
Watch yourself well
Just wait for the bell
Don't walk anywhere without a friend
Don't defend your beliefs just pretend
Not being one of us I don't recommend
Because we will give you a bitter end

Chorus

SASHA VILLARREAL, AGE 15

This is a song that I wrote at the WriteGirl Songwriting Workshop. I was inspired by a sticky note on the back of a chair. On it, another girl had written, "Grey Girl."

Grey Girl

Colors fall from my eyes.
Blue tinted tears
streak down my face.
What is this feeling?
Why does my heart race?

As the darkness begins to fade,
the once colorless world
turns into sparkling rays
making me no longer
the girl who was grey.

Always carry
something to write
with, because
writing can
happen anywhere
at anytime.

12

EXTRA UNORDINARY GIRL

Challenges

Personal Statement

Home was a museum of broken glass where pain could be inflicted on me at any time. I left last June. The air I breathe no longer smells like bitterness. I fought my whole life to get out of nowhere and go somewhere, to reach light at the end of the darkest aisle. I'm working, fighting and growing. I write every day on my soft mattress at the group home I live in. In a week I'll start therapy. I finally feel the outcome of the battle is in my hands. It's not the same fight anymore – now I can win. I can succeed; I feel it. It's so close; it's almost mine but not quite. My life feels like a movie, with the sequence of things being so dramatic, sometimes I peer back at the specter of my old self and smile. I feel I can save her. I can save me, like everything is going to be okay.

I think my life has taught me to survive, to go on despite adversity. As a student I know education is one of the few things that can permanently change my circumstances. So I must fight for it. I love learning. Every class I take makes me a better artist even if initially I don't understand it or it's hard for me to grasp. When I learn it gives me a broader view of the world around me and changes my perspective. As a little girl I never thought I'd be here. I never thought my life could improve so drastically. But I think I've taught my old self, the little girl in me, that no matter where you come from, you can go anywhere you want to.

I created a simpler version of this poem when I was in sixth grade. Years later, I decided to expand upon my original ideas.

Freedom Calls

Leaving them behind was the worst part,
The memories he missed,
Anniversaries, birthdays,
Yet it was his duty to protect those beyond his borders.

He had sailed every sea's bend,
The steel frame of the ship embracing him like a trusted friend,
Protecting him from harm.

The whisper of the waves comforted him,
He had been accustomed to his duty, fond almost.
The sea had raised him,
Shaping him into the man his daughter admired.

As the waves engulfed the desolate rocks
The moon reached its highest peak.
The man was nowhere to be found;
He will not be there tomorrow.

Graduating early wasn't easy, but it made me even more determined to follow my dreams.

To Everyone Who Said I Couldn't Make It

They say I'm not bright.
They say I have no future.
Some may call me a "last chance" student.
Well with all due respect, Ma'am,
let me paint you a clearer picture.

I heard a rumor on the street
that people were making fun of me
because I chose a path
a bit different from the cookie-cutter lifestyle.

I have dealt with issues
that I don't feel the need to disclose.
I stand here today, a stronger person despite you.
I will not succumb to your petty little comments about my schooling.
I made the honor roll twice.
I refuse to back down.
I have the courage to prove to people like you,
that I can make it,
that I am something.
I won't be forced to work for minimum wage,
a cookie-cutter lifestyle.
Because I'll be the girl
going down in history
as the one
who made something of herself.

Sometimes the hardest
experiences can be the
greatest stories.

When you run out of ideas, write from your dreams, fears and biggest nightmares. Just write.

This piece is about an 11-mile hike that proved to me how strong I am, and how strong I've been.

Eleven-Mile Enlightenment

It's a mountain, and mountains are meant to be climbed. I stand on a patch of grass, shield my eyes from the sun as I stare at its grandeur. Right in front of me, one great big symbol. The metaphor of all metaphors. After years of sports injuries and surgeries on both my legs, everything has been a mountain. Standing, walking, driving, working, hiking.

In front of me looms Castro Peak, with jagged ridges and thorny chaparral. At the top, I might get a view of the ocean. I could play it safe, protect myself. Sit cross-legged in the grass and passively admire its splendid existence. Or trade my comfort for guaranteed pain...and a slight chance at victory. So I choose pain. Slowly I walk, thinking only about my footsteps creating a steady heartbeat. Pain develops in my knees. I focus on the sweet smell of sage and the big blue flowers lining the trail. Finally I reach the top of a mountain I've been eyeing for miles and discover Castro is miles away. I trudge along.

I no longer see any other day-hikers. Just backpackers, carrying a weekend's worth of supplies. I shake my water bottle. Almost empty. Dozens of just-around-the-bends later, I scramble my wobbly legs to the peak. I pause and scan the coastline. The rolling fog of Oxnard, the sparkling waves of Malibu, the Santa Monica Ferris wheel, a distant Catalina Island. I am stunned.

I grab an apple from my backpack, and I take a juicy bite. Tears fill my eyes. Although some mountains are deceptively high, accomplishment can be overwhelmingly delicious.

BRIANNA MEJIA, AGE 13

I'm the oldest of six kids and felt for a long time that I had too much responsibility. I feel better about it now, but I used to resent it.

You Can't Ask Me

You can't ask me to raise your children
to be that nurturing and mature
to be as loving and patient as you are
shield them from life or make mine all about them

You can't ask me to always put them before myself
to be that selfless, that perfect
give them my everything

And just because
you can't ask me never to leave them
doesn't mean I won't still be there
doesn't mean I won't still love them, or you

JESSICA LEWIS, AGE 14

Boundaries

With nature
comes limitations.
    Boundaries.

Boundaries in our lives. Every day
they limit our power, strangle
our imagination
and choke our desire.

The cruelest illusions.

But loosen your senses
and conquer your fears.
Your boundaries can be
    defeated.

*I wrote this piece in a WriteGirl workshop
that had to do with emigration, so I wrote
about how I am a foster child and how
I move from home to home.*

Four Walls

Four walls.
Five, if you count the ceiling.
They always vary in size
and location.

Always different colors,
cracks,
stains,
windows.

Always four walls to shield me.
Always four walls surround me.
Four is a good number
a safe number.

I don't need a castle
just four walls.
I might not have a family at the moment
but I'm okay with my four walls.

I wrote this when I felt like I needed to be somebody else – an ordinary girl.

I Am an Extra Unordinary Girl

Sometimes I wish I could be an ordinary girl. Every day when I walk through the hallway of my school, I feel everyone is staring, that I'm sticking out. I just want to be one in the crowd. I don't want special treatment, I don't need sympathy. I can do what an ordinary kid can do. I just want to be like other "normal" kids.

I want to have it easy. I don't want to get extra time on tests or go to bed early so I can stand the next day. My life has always been about doctor's appointments and "What's wrong with Noa?" I watched my wonderful cousins prance around perfectly, but whenever I pranced around, I would fall flat on my face. I don't know why this means so much to me. I have disabilities – so what? I mean, it's not like somebody died.

In the mornings I dream of the boys I want to ask me out, and the people I wish would talk to me, if they only knew that I loved them. But at the lunch table, I sit alone, waiting for someone to come talk to me. In the light comes the darkness – my self-esteem goes down a hundred points. I suppose, though, in the darkness comes the light – I realize that I can do whatever I want, that I am gorgeous and that nothing can hold me back.

I'm not an ordinary girl, but no one really is. I don't have to hide. I can conquer the world, because I'm not an ordinary girl – I am way better. I'm Noa, proud to be the extra unordinary girl.

13

JUST BENEATH
THE SURFACE

Growing Up

I dedicate this poem to India Radfar, one of the most inspiring women I've ever met, because, no matter how many times I told her I disliked it, she coaxed me into thinking it wasn't as dumb as I originally thought it was.

Molecules

I feel empty.
I'm waiting by the door for a package that was never ordered
There's nothing coming in my near future.
I feel alone.
Every soul that I speak to only acknowledges me to the slightest.
Who's there to save me?
Other people find help
What makes me different?

A fuse set off by the mere movement of molecules
The daily grind grinds my gears exceptionally quickly
The buzz and hum of an average request to others
is the screech and halt of all cooperation for me

When I grow up I'd like to be a rocket that flies to outer space
No matter the weight I could still take flight
No inquiries are asked of something that knows the universe on a first name basis
God and I would exchange pleasantries up there
But I wouldn't stop for anything except the end of everything
Where space turns to light, light turns to dark, and teenage girl turns to rocket.

ERICA W. JAMIESON, MENTOR

Bell-Bottoms

My first pair of bell-bottoms was a gift from my father. I was used to my father gifting my mother with clothes, but the pants in the colorful Bonwit's box, this time, were mine. They made me feel grown up. When I tried them on, I felt like I had fallen right out of the fashion magazines my mother read at the beauty shop. It was 1968, and the first time I wore my new pants was to school on Monday morning, so I could show them off during Show and Tell.

They were creamy white with bright rows of embroidery at the hem, different from the plaid kilt skirts and blue knit sweaters I usually wore. Show and Tell took place with all of the children seated in a circle around Mrs. Zoomo in the story alcove of our classroom. When it was my turn, I stood and twirled in my new bell-bottom pants letting the hems float up in a great swoosh of fabric. Mrs. Zoomo interrupted the children's clapping with a loud clearing of her throat. "Young ladies," she said, "should not be seen out of the house in long pants. It is unladylike."

When I got home that day, I took off my new bell-bottoms with the rows of colorful stitching and never wore them again.

Mrs. Zoomo hounded me for years to return to her class. She had something for me she would say if she saw me in the halls. I finally returned just before I left Dewey Elementary for good. She handed me a rolled up piece of construction paper on which I had drawn a stick figure in bell-bottom pants with bright lines of orange and blue and red at the hem. The stick figure had long curly hair and was standing by a tree with the sun shining brightly, a bird soaring in the sky. "I've saved this for you all these years," she said. And so she had.

Since the National Center for the Preservation of Democracy tells the story of many immigrant families, we were asked to think about a change or transition in our own lives and to tell that story through an object.

But I Have to Take It

The man at the post office grunts.
"This one's 60 pounds. What the heck's in here?"
That would be my sewing machine.
Doubt floods my veins.
But I have to take it.
Why am I taking it?
Across a continent, as far as one can go from east to west.
What does one take for a journey like this?
Clothes, sheets, laptop – they all seem obvious.
Logical. Necessary.
But my sewing machine?
Ridiculous. Unnecessary.
But I have to take it.

My mom sewed, as her mother did before her.
My mom taught me to sew. She gave me this machine.
And now she is gone.
And I am moving on.
Moving away.
5,000 miles.
I have to take it.

It arrives on the opposite coast with just a small crack on one corner of the case.
I had planned to stay for just two months…it's been almost ten years.

The sewing machine stayed, too.

A Journey

A journey
is a lifelong trip
to become strong
mature

many people
inspire
or discourage
But don't stop

dream big
don't fail
be brave
fight on

I wrote this piece during my first day volunteering in the In-Schools Program. As a WriteGirl alumna, it was surreal, being a mentor and experiencing the other side of being a part of WriteGirl.

Of Things Called Life

Past experiments, led to
comparisons of success and failure.
Projections of what could be
and what is.

Present, waiting and working
and building,
connecting,
and noticing growth.

This is a poem in a spontaneous format that was inspired by how we express denial of reality.

Denial

My world is perfect.
Perfect this…there…that.
Everything is perfect!
Hello! Oh yes, that's it!

> *Wait*
> *that's not there, No.*
> *No, that can't go there, no, no, no.*
> *You don't go there, No.*
> *You don't fit. Goodbye.*

Break, Crash, Crumble. My world isn't real.

> *The snowflakes in the air.*
> *The springtime.*
> *World, why did you go?*

My time, I wasted it, I spent it.
Time was currency, debting me
from the realities that I didn't like.

> *Fantasy. Yes, yes, That's it,*
> *that's it! Return.*
> *Relapse.*
> *Yes, truth: Deny it.*

When I was growing up, my friends and I were drawn to a mysterious iron sculpture with inscriptions that we would try to decipher.

Pedaling Toward the Apocalypse

We ride our Schwinns over drying mounds of mud and granite that taper off into the streets like fat, sleeping snakes. The road rises and falls with the contours of the desert and the gullies carved by fast-moving water of quick summer storms.

We leave behind afternoon reruns about three-hour cruises gone awry, zany red-heads, and Captain Kirk. We pass the tree fort cut into green Palo Verde branches, and the empty battlefield with its weedy ruts and endless supply of dirt clod weaponry. We pass the empty pink mansion on the hill that keeps us out with its tall fence and unscalable steep cliffs. We hear the echo of hammers against two-by-fours and pedal around the trucks of the men who use them. When they leave, we'll run through the labyrinth of newly laid pipes and up the skeleton stairs they've made.

We discuss the merits of tales carried on the twilight bark of grade school rumors: the Pop Rocks that killed Mikey, the Clackers that maimed. We ride with hands in the air, mimicking cheers done by other girls, chanting in the rhyming cadence we've heard them use, copying their precision movements and rigid hand claps, slapping our thighs covered in thick polyester gym shorts. With twinges of hope and envy, we…Go. Bananas. B-A-N-A-N-A-S.

We come to a spot set back from the quiet, ranch-style homes and drop our bikes in the dirt next to a rusted metal box that's taller than all of us. Rambling messages of doom cover dozens of panels welded together to make up the walls. We trace the words "Death Box" printed there, and run our fingers over weld points that look like rough scars. We read the inscriptions aloud, ponder their meaning, press our ears against the sides and listen, but find only heat and the smell of iron.

Take your journal to somewhere you have never been before. New places can bring out new ideas.

Write until you can
convince the universe
to swallow its secrets
and spit back poetry
and fiction.

I wrote this piece thinking about my family and the battles in my life. I wanted to show how I felt when everyone seemed to be pushing me.

Bricks of Anger

He wants to go back in time,
look back at our mistakes,
slowly learn from them.

She wants to live for the future,
prepare for what's ahead,
leave behind the burden.

I don't know what I want.
Heavy bricks of anger
gather on my shoulders.
I want to shake it all off.
It's too much to handle.

Everything in my heart coils up,
twisting and bending
until it pushes my limits,
and I break and shatter.
I let go of everything inside me.
But even after that, I still have those bricks –
bricks of anger.

This is from a short story that was inspired by visiting my childhood home. I went with the intention of reconnecting with my father after three years of estrangement.

Going Home (An Excerpt)

As she walked into the house she felt sick yet oddly, uncomfortably, at home. It smelled like old cologne and stuffiness. Her father quickly excused himself as he complained that he lost his glasses. He must find them before they could leave.

She slowly walked into the kitchen – the same kitchen that she frequented as a child for a midnight snack or to watch her mother or father as they made dinner. Always separately. Never together. The kitchen seemed so much smaller. Tiny almost. As if it were a kitchen in a dollhouse or for a little gnome that lived in a cottage in the middle of nowhere. Not a normal kitchen. She felt like a giant standing in the center atop the grimy linoleum. Had the kitchen always been this small? Or had she just grown more than she thought she had? Or both? As a child it seemed insurmountable. Like a vast ocean where she could barely keep herself afloat or an epic mountain that she could never see herself climbing as she stood, feet bare, tippy toed, fingers outstretched to their full extent reaching for the peanut butter on the top middle shelf, before her father came along and grabbed it for her. Her knight in shining armor. Her hero. Then, not now.

As she got older that fairy tale image faded. She realized that her concept of "Dad" was this man that she never bothered to understand. But, alas, as she grew up she came to the realization that her father, like her mother, was a mere mortal. No perfection or powers graced their bodies or spirits. But as a young girl she believed they could fly if they really wanted to, and if they did, they would take her with them.

SARAH THOMAS FAZELI, MENTOR

Whenever I make, eat or see a homemade birthday cake, I think of my mom. Birthday cakes were and are her realm, totem, thing. They connect me to my childhood, and our relationship.

My Mother's Mantra

I hope nothing *really* bad ever happens to you,
my mother rolled her eyes when I was six
and skinned my knee and wailed,
doubling over in dramatic agony.
I threw myself around her bare feet,
curled around them like our old, heavy cat.
But she had already taken a step, and
tripped over my size 6x body and Buster Brown sandals.
Sunday coupons flew like the shiny paper birds
trapped in my Mary Poppins snowglobe.
They floated down in slow, lazy whorls;
perforated petals across the kitchen floor.

Now, slicing my 30th birthday cake, I nick
my pinky finger. I whisper-swear, and
quick! nurse it to my mouth.
My mother takes the knife from my hand,
seamlessly resumes the ritual.
Cutting perfect triangles, she places one in front of me and sighs,
I hope nothing *really* bad ever happens to you.
I sweep my cut finger along the cake's creamy curve,
the white Betty Crocker frosting, a brief bandage
before I raise it against my lips and tongue.
The choke-sweet, sugar sting tempers the iron taste of blood.

I wanted to try my hand at the nonfiction genre this year, and in thinking about recent life events I found that the most interesting thing that happened to me was that I got a daring new haircut.

Just the Tips

What was a head full of fiery red hair over the summer had become a faded mess of pink fuzz that reached my chest by the winter. It was time for a trip to the salon. "Just the tips," I always said. This time though, I had a secret agenda; one that I knew Mami wouldn't agree with. That is, unless she had just finished dinner and wasn't feeling guilty for eating too many tortillas. This was always the best time to ask for something in my family. It was on one such night that she agreed to take me to the salon saying, "Ya es tiempo." Out of her view, I smiled so big that my eyes met my cheeks.

At the salon, the soft, peach lighting and plush, velvety cushions had me feeling optimistic that my plan to remove much more than "just the tips" might actually work. I'd spent the last six months yearning for a mature, short hairstyle that would relieve me from the scrunchy that made me a child. I had to have a bob – just like Katie Holmes. Shaking with excitement, I showed the hairdresser a photo of what I wanted. While Mami waited patiently in the salon's lobby, the hairdresser went to work. Puffs of pink hair fell to the floor all around me.

When she put down her scissors and turned my chair to face the mirror, I swear I didn't recognize the girl staring back at me. She was stunning with short, black hair and pretty pink tips. When my mother came up behind me moments later, her eyes were wide with a look that said, *Lupe, what have you done?* Just below the surface of her expression, however, was the realization that her youngest daughter was growing up.

If you need something to
write about, go outside,
take a breath and let
images flood your paper
in words.

14
BROWN SUGAR MORNINGS

Food

This piece was inspired by the shape of a candy cane and the magic of writing.

Candy Cane

I do not know all of what she said,
a sandglass spilling out its contents, the winding words dispersing like stones.
I remember them falling from her mouth, weightless droplets of sound,
two words, illuminated above all the rest: candy cane.

Something ignited inside me, the pencil clutched in my hand,
maniacally moving across the paper.
I began a journey, excavating that flickering light she'd planted inside me,
a faint and sensational mirage, like sea frost kissing the cliff of my toes.

I reached out – tiny splayed fingers reached for what was intangible,
lifted like fluttering leaves by the tendrils and drawstrings
of my own imagination,
    scarlet vines of sugary canes,
    the twisting insignia of barber shops,
    the world,
    unriddled and decoded.

I raised my head, intoxicated with the dazzling words before me,
planets and flowers and souls and the universe all designed,
embroidered and fastened.

The pages closed, the reverie died and buried itself.
Like a phoenix, new ones would awaken me,
make me rise from blowing ashes,
spiraling like the ribbons of a candy cane.

I wrote this piece during the WriteGirl Journalism Workshop at the Los Angeles Times headquarters. There was a recipe-writing experiment, and I wrote about all the elements in my life as a second-generation Asian American.

Recipe for My All-American Life

A writing pad
Bundles of pens
Dishes of half-eaten seafood paella
A dog-eared red envelope filled with incense
Black tights and strewn tutus
Thumping beats of '90s pop music groups
Bowls of salsa and chips
A bookcase of Jane Austen novels
A camera filled with memories gathered
From all walks of life
Mixed together, stirring with no avail
An All-American Life no less

This excerpt is from a piece about a food-related routine. My dogs have very strong personalities and I love including them in my writing.

Saturday Brunches

It's too early on a Saturday morning, and I wake up to the sound of her whimper. Sometimes, depending on the weather and how cold she is or how much she ate the night before, she follows these whimpers with a louder and more annoying cage rattle. It's a sound equivalent to a caged bird trying to stretch her feathers in a cage too small. But this is no bird, and the kennel is actually a size too big. And then, depending on how cold I am or how much I ate the night before, I get up.

My jailbird, a brown and white Chihuahua/Jack Russell mix, calms down as she hears my feet hit the hardwood floor. We head to the kitchen in silence, soon joined by another hungry four-legged patron (a black and white Shih-Tzu) who launches off the bed and hits the floor with a clumsy thud. She only gets up for food. At the kitchen, I divvy up the kibble in two red plastic bowls and separate the two brats on opposite ends of the apartment because they both take their meals too seriously.

I then start my internal timer because in about two minutes, someone will be done eating and will try to steal the other's food. But in these same two minutes I have peace and stare into the open refrigerator to figure out today's morning specialty. Pancakes and what? Pancakes and what? Eggs? I love eggs. Omelet? Where's the cheese? There's the cheese. Ooooh, bacon. I pile the ingredients on the counter.

No cold bowl of cereal, no large cup of coffee, and no plateful of emails to answer today. I look down and find two sets of eyes staring up at me. Yes, today will be much different.

I volunteered at a WriteGirl summer poetry workshop. The prompt was, "The Other Side of the Door." My relative, Sylvia, who founded a famous soul food restaurant in Harlem, had died the day before.

The Other Side of the Door

Nothing is as good as crispy, juicy, savory fried chicken,
the Sunday and holiday food of my youth,
served with potato salad, sweet with relish, and collard greens.
I haven't eaten it in years.
Bad for your heart, they say.
Sylvia, who passed away yesterday
appeared on the other side of the door
with my mother, who passed away years ago.
Sylvia mirrored my gap teeth with her grin, saying,
"I ate and cooked soul food all my life.
Soul food didn't kill me.
It gave me life, a living, and Wikipedia fame.
I did not die sick, I died 86,
curious about the other side of the door.
My food is the heart of Harlem.
My restaurant is the heart of my family.
Don't abandon soul food, woman child,
that's heart trouble of another kind,
hardening the arteries of spirit and connection.
Feeling a little lost?
Fry up some chicken and make a tasty potato salad
in remembrance of me and your ancestors.
Reconnect."

Perfect Day

In the morning, I smell sweet warm Belgian waffles with cinnamon - it's as if I can feel the waffles giving me a hug. I wrap myself in the delicious air and watch as it dances around me. I taste the fruit alongside the waffles, the sourness of the strawberries, bitter but luscious. I savor every last piece of the soft waffles, consumed by the taste. I can almost hear my stomach thanking me.

As I finish, I continue with my day and head out the door to the beach. I love to watch the waves crash onto the shore. I sit on the ground and press my fingertips on the roughness of the sand. I lie on the ground and absorb the sunshine on my face. I relax and watch as the world goes by.

Chocolate goes really well with telling stories.

AUNYE SCOTT-ANDERSON, AGE 17

My grandmother used to make me drink tea with Cayenne pepper to help with sinus issues in the wintertime. I drink it as often as possible now and, every time I make it, I think of her.

Cayenne Tea

Memories are transfixed in people, places and things,
trapped, undiscovered by their hosts until the revelation.

I remember…
Embers, hot and curious, easing down my throat,
a sip of autumn personified.
Red flecks bewitched by white ceramic
cling and sting the roof of my mouth,
terribly, enjoyably strange.
I remember Cayenne Tea on brown sugar mornings
when noses dripped lazily and the
sun rolled its rays away to weep.
Carnation Milk and Ovaltine,
her wide lap hugged my plump pre-pubescent frame
like an egg encasing its precious yolk.
I remember her, my fragment of history,
my beloved piece of the past,
my grandma.
I remember how she poured
ample love-honey in my tea-mug
to cure winter morning sniffles.
I taste her in the Cayenne Tea I brew myself,
in the love-honey I've always been enamored with.
I sip slowly,
allowing reminiscences to settle on my tongue.

RIB-BREAKING HUGS

Friendship

SAMMY CASE, AGE 15

Throughout my sophomore year of high school, I have encountered many new people and made many new friendships.

A Place in My Ribs

I have let certain people creep into my ribs
Through the gaps between the bones;
When they started to tickle me
And laughter erupted from my throat
I knew they had earned a place to stay
And that I would be seeing them very soon.

Don't think or all your ideas will sink.

LAUREN RODRIGUEZ, AGE 16

I wrote this piece about my old best friend because I really miss her and the way things used to be.

Lost and Found

I lost a friendship
And the purple sock with bananas had lost its match.

I lost my best friend
And found myself left with an acquaintance.

I lost the rib-breaking hugs
And found half-hearted smiles and muttered hellos.

I lost the late night talks
And found all my thoughts bottled up.

I gave up looking for the purple sock with bananas
And I gave up on you, too.

Life's Promises: A Misunderstanding Generation (An Excerpt)

On January the 16th, around 8:53 pm, I lost my true best friend. My universe tilted slightly. Three months have passed, but that night is still raw in my head, and I can't forget about him.

Betrayal is bittersweet, he needed to hear the truth from me...

It felt like just yesterday when he gave me the letter and I pulled him close, never wanting to let the moment go, shutting my eyes tight, hoping in some way to stop all time. He promised in the letter he would always be here for me. He promised it would be me, forever, and not her.

Now our friendship had disintegrated into pieces, the flames calmed, and all emotion has vanished. I used to have a best friend. Grown-ups have told me I won't see or remember more than half the people I went to high school with, but for now I'll wake up every morning and enjoy the day – with my so-called best friends.

The assignment was to write a poem based on a certain item;
the outcome was a poem about an old friendship and a gift
that she gave me.

Goodbye Bracelet

I thought it was priceless
Something mundane
A silver chain, my link
A heart charm, my love
A bracelet, my friendship

I never thought I'd let it go
I never thought I'd throw it away
But then one day it was no longer just a chain
It was a prison
It tied me to suffering, to insecurity

My plan of escape was to break it
Slowly weather it away with time
I tried to start anew and find myself again
I indulged myself with new jewelry –
Jubilant crystal necklaces, flitting feather earrings
Even new bracelets
Each as unique and wonderful as the next

As time went by my rusted chains loosened
I broke free
I keep the remnants safe
Close to my heart to remember,
To acknowledge the person I once was

I met a new friend at a workshop, and we instantly connected. I wrote this for her, telling her how grateful I am for her friendship.

Peas from Different Pods

You and I,
peas from different pods.

Blue eyes,
brown eyes,
a pair of girls lost at sea

for far too long…
for childhood lost…
For all the tears we shed.

We drift no more, releasing our shells,
safe at last.

What lies ahead are clearer days,
happier notes.
Hand in hand, two girls
smiling at the dawn.

Shining eyes look into mine.
I am fulfilled

with love.

I had a childhood friend who constantly told stories from her imaginary world, and I never forgot this particular one.

Delusional Love

Ashley
Full of vibrant lies
With eyes that tell the truth
Yet doubt fills my mind
While my heart is filled with belief inside
As her lips weave a story
She speaks of her lover
The Raccoon
Her butterfly necklace clings to her chest
Symbolizing their everlasting love
How and why, my eyes seemed to ask
And with a smirk
Ms. Ashley simply replied, "It's true"
Nothing discouraged her
No proper dosage of reality brought her down
For between this world and hers
There was no boundary
For her and the raccoon
There was only love.

Write your words as if the reader is right in front of you and the two of you are sharing a bottle of pop!

Don't take
adjectives
for granted.

Venture to different
surroundings for
different stories.

"A cloud jumper?" June asked during physics. "You're kidding, right?" I shook my head. "I'm serious, Emma, what are you gonna be when you grow up?"

"Well, maybe not a cloud jumper. Maybe a frog whisperer. Or a fairy."

June rolled her eyes. "Do you at least know where you want to go for college?"

I shrugged and tapped my pencil on the desk. "I dunno. Why, what's your big plan?"

"I'm going to be a brain surgeon. I already have a medical internship for this summer. My top choice is Johns Hopkins, but my next choices are…" Honestly, I lost her after that.

June snapped her fingers in my face. "Emma, we'll be applying for college in a couple months. How can you not know anything about your future?"

I smirked, and her eyebrows twisted. "Trust me," I replied, "I know as much about the future as you do."

I never thought writing about such a serious topic could make me giggle so much.

Not Thorough

Thoreau once wrote that hell itself could be contained within a spark. Think of that next time you're roasting marshmallows, striking a match, or warming your feet by a fireplace. Suffering souls make your toes tingle. But the burning question is, where's heaven? What do we do with the directions to the wrong destination? No one wants to know how to get to the where they don't want to go. Thoreau, should I balance the equation you have given me? Finish the analogy? Hell is to a spark as heaven is to…a water droplet? Thank God I'm on the swim team.

Always keep a pencil or pen with some paper next to your bed because when you have an idea worth writing, who needs sleep?!

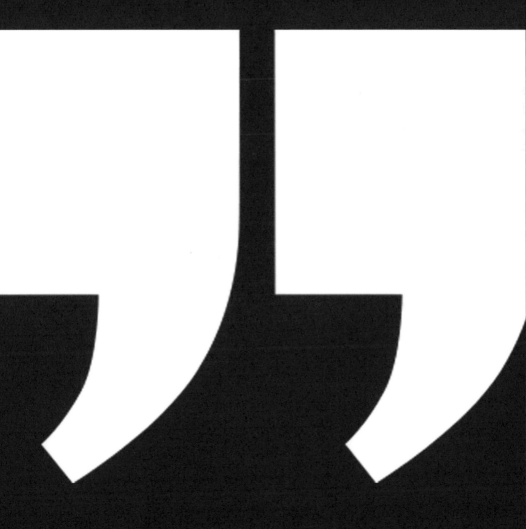

NATHALIE MADRIGAL, AGE 17

This poem was inspired by the movie Into the Wild.

Coexistence

Come with me on a journey
of self-realization.

You mustn't doubt me.
Proceed without hesitation to a world

like no other.
Exotic and beautiful
everyone coexists
and everyone gets along
with each other.

No barriers or walls, or materialistic possessions
nothing
but the calls of nature and happy celebrations
where we are one
with the moon
and the stars
and the sun.

Like clouds floating above the big blue.
Worry free.

Don't you wish that was you?

My favorite band, Mindless Behavior, inspired this piece because they helped me find my true self.

The Rebel

The one that sits in back of the class
The one who doesn't listen

He's scared, confused, hurt, frustrated
Smart

He gets picked on for being himself
Tries to change, but it doesn't work
He cries out for help

Can't get out of his own thoughts
It's like he's in a locked box

DANIELA FLORES-RODRIGUEZ, AGE 15

I wrote this piece to show how I picture literature in my head when I'm reading a book.

Literature

Words float off the page
To create fantastical images
Wonderful worlds collide

Inky battles play out in my head
Love stories capture my soul
Adventure glides in a circle of words

Time whirls backward
Dreams of ball gowns become reality
Names become eternal

In mere silence
I see whole lives
In the background of literature

Read everything — even things you normally don't. You never know what you'll find.

This piece was inspired by a late night visit to downtown Los Angeles.

Nightlife

A plethora of beauty surrounds me,
I close my eyes
to see its fluorescent energy.
I listen carefully
to hear its heart beat.
Night life.

LISA BEEBE, MENTOR

A poem about acupuncture, and Los Angeles, and loving my dog.

The Big One

If an earthquake comes
The big one, I mean
It will come while you are getting acupuncture

You'll have needles between your toes
Needles in your shins, knees, breast bone
You won't know what to do
You'll wonder about your apartment
Pray that your dog is ok
I need to get home, you'll think; I need to get these needles out

You will think about love
As the city shakes and shudders, and parts of it fall

When you find your way home
After a drive with no street lights and too many sirens
Your dog will be happy to see you
He will jump up, excited, as if to say, "Things fell! Things broke!"
You will sit on the floor and hug him
Because that's how it works
The world shakes
The world breaks
And we hug it back together
Together

This is the beginning of a fiction story, inspired by the first line, which was overheard in a nearby conversation during a meeting with my mentee.

Mackie's Farm

My cousin had a suicidal dog. A real idiotic mutt named Buster – so creative – who used to climb onto the back of his dad's pickup truck when it was doing 30 miles an hour on the road into town. Stupid thing must have fallen out three or four times that summer. Broke a different leg each time. Mackie thought it was hilarious.

"Keep the darn dog on his leash!" his dad would yell every time we climbed into the back for a ride to get groceries and ice cream. Mackie would swear he would, but as soon as we turned onto that road, he'd unhook Buster and watch him run around the truck bed excited.

"You wanna see where we been, don'tcha Buster? You wanna see?" And he'd tap on the rear door and egg him on until the dumb mutt started scratching his way up the back. If I ever reached over to try to save him from his foolish demise, Mackie would just elbow me in the chest. "Mind your own business, JJ!" He always knew how to hit the same spot in my chest, which sucked because the previous bruise usually wasn't healed before he hit it again.

I hated those summers, trapped on the farm with Mackie and his dad while my parents hopped around the globe. They were engineering professors at the local university with a research focus on water purification in third world nations. They took a group of grad students to various countries every summer to build aqueducts and wells and whatnot. They never took me, because they didn't want me "gallivanting around those dirty, dangerous places."

So instead, they sent me to a different third world nation – Mackie's farm.

At the WriteGirl Flash Workshop at the National Center for the Preservation of Democracy, we were asked to write a poem about a physical object.

Shielding Shades

I grope in my purse
They must be there somewhere
Days, months of training myself to carry them with me wherever I go
I sigh with relief when my fingers grasp plastic
and I slide my giant black sunglasses onto my face
Only the uninitiated would think these glasses solely shield my eyes
from the sun
No, these glasses do more than that
They shield my Self from this world
From the bright sun, bright lights, dark secrets and constant chaos that
is L.A.
With them on, I look like I belong
I am protected.

MCKENZIE GIVENS, AGE 17

I wrote this piece while backpacking in Alaska during the summer. The landscape was pristine and remote.

have you seen the mountains?

have you seen the mountains?
the way the Earth bares both soul and bones to the Sky above?
she is dangerous and vulnerable. unashamed.
the incontrovertible queen of an undying age.
and have you seen the way he loves her?
the way he hugs all her curves and lifts her into the ether?
their love is sublime. trancelike and immortal.
unstained but not unchanged.
by the passage of time.

we are but a witness to their romance,
transient residents in their miraculous instant.
it is an honor to perceive them,
a privilege to cast our bones between them.

This piece stemmed from an exhibit of letters home I saw at the WriteGirl Poetry Workshop at the National Center for the Preservation of Democracy.

I Am My Own Home

In Calistoga there are stars – thousands of them and each one I had forgotten. I'm exhausted by the time we get there. Ten to midnight and all the muscles in my body ache for bed.

DJ plays dubstep the entire way from L.A., so my head is spinning, my heart left south, in Silverlake, our little home with the front lawn and friendly neighborhood cats. Somehow Calistoga has become a haven for me after all these years. Two nights away will do me good, I keep thinking/saying. Two nights in town will clear my head, charge me up, rejuvenate me. Send me back into the world ready to go. I'll be more prepared this time, I think.

In the morning my mother wakes me up, opening the door just a crack, like she can't believe it's me. She's done this since I was a child. Our secret knocks on thin walls.

But lately wherever I am is home. Not just where my stuff is, not just where my people are, or some one person or bed in particular. I am my own home, lately – my things strewn across rooms all over California – jewelry and shoes, notebooks and paper slips getting lost in the shuffle of it all. Home is wherever I am at the moment. I am transient; I belong nowhere and everywhere at once.

I need to go home, he says. *You are home*, she reminds him.

MARISSA CHRISTIANSEN, MENTOR

I wrote this at a WriteGirl workshop. It was an "in the garden" experiment.

The Path

I stood in a garden, lush and beautiful. The sun glistened on dewy petals. But the clouds came too often, the beauty of the garden was only so for those fleeting moments in between lightning. The rain fell so hard it ripped petals from their stalks.

I escaped, seeking refuge in a new garden, a smaller garden. The foliage there was different, but with a larger abundance of blooms. The blooms weathered the storms and were happier, fuller and brighter for it. There were storms on the horizon; ominous thunderheads loomed with the threat of familiar destruction. I was frightened. And so I ran – not out of the garden, but through it, for the back of it revealed an undiscovered path. The path led to a new world of gardens beyond.

I wrote a series of poems based on NYC subway rats.

eternally, rat

drops of rainwater sift
through the grate above
like thousands of sharp little choices
soaking me in *now* –
tick ahead, shuffle back
        take the bridge
take the tunnel
dirt-soaked moments
in constant frenzy
make my scabbed coat glisten
in concussive beads
        and so I shake
off no escape
     from this strange climate
unloading the weight
shake off like a pinch
to confirm a dream
the most direct course
winding thick
between walls
of *this*.

While volunteering in the WriteGirl In-Schools Program, we worked with the girls to write about a place that holds good memories.

Clearwater, Florida

Hunting for starfish, seashells…the smell of the salt water ocean mixed with the smell of my sunscreen. The waves crashed. The seagulls screeched because my sister was throwing popcorn up into the air. "Stop that! Look out below!" I laughed with my sister at the hermit crabs scurrying across the sand.

In my memory, I can hear Aunt Anne's voice telling me the names of the shells as we walked along the surf line, picking up each new souvenir: cat's paw, jingles, turkey wing, bleeding tooth.

After the cold New York weather, we hated to leave the warm sandy beach. The smell of Solarcaine being slathered onto red skin after our showers – as indelible a memory as the sand dollars and starfish in our suitcases.

I just moved to El Sereno, and for the first time, I have a garden.

Ballard Street

I think I've pulled up a few things I should have left in the earth, and from the kitchen window, I can see a few fast-growing, spiky-leaved shoots that really need to go. I'm trying to learn how to identify a weed from a keeper plant, but I have no experience with this at all.

Since I have some cactus on the hill, I bought a pair of special "thorn-proof" garden gloves that have thick grey leather all the way up to the elbow. I didn't exactly plan to buy them, but the hardware store was closing, and there were delicious round neon price tags on everything. I couldn't resist. I envision myself fearlessly pruning my cactus. Do cacti even need pruning?

I also bought a bag of mulch – they only had large, 3.0 cubic feet bags that I couldn't lift by myself. I'm not sure what to do with mulch, yet, but it was a good price, I think. Mulch sounds like something experienced gardeners use. I'm fast-tracking myself.

There are five large agave plants in a cluster – grand blue-green mandalas, unspiraling toward the sun. I broke off some of the dead leaves, clad in my new leather gloves, and found some miniature milky green spirals growing underneath. I am an explorer, an excavator. I don't own a shovel yet, but I'll get there.

Take your story idea for a walk around the block and let the trees, flowers and your neighbor's dog inspire you with more ideas.

When I think about my childhood, I am struck by the absurd juxtaposition of the small and commonplace with the large and strange. I grew up in another time and place entirely: Budapest, under Communism.

Titans

I loved playing at Lenin's feet. In my defense, I was only eight. He was an enormous bronze statue atop a pedestal on "Parade Plaza," a pedestrian expanse paved with elegant square tiles sandwiched between a busy boulevard and the verdant City Park. Lenin's arm was stretched out, his palm turned sideways as if hailing a cab. This was no easy task on that stretch of road.

It took my dad and me 15 minutes on Saturday mornings to ride our bikes there. I dreaded pedaling on the street, and my dad had to push my bike at the crosswalk. Once there, I could ride around in figure eights, then climb up next to Lenin's shoes and under the folds of his trousers where I'd play with my plastic dolls. It was a nice, shady spot.

Lenin shared the plaza with the "Memorial of the Republic," a colossal, strapping young workman taking one giant leap, presumably into a more promising future, with arms raised as if to throw a javelin while brandishing a swath of bronze cloth: either a flag or a superhero cape. His inclined pedestal was rather perfect for a slide.

I was not the only child enchanted with these fantastical creatures. A small gaggle was content to play pretend or the occasional hide-and-seek on Saturdays.

Long after Communism fell, when I returned to visit, the statues had been moved to "Memento Park" in the outskirts. Curious tourists pay a few dollars to marvel at the monuments of a bygone era, preserved by the wisdom to remember rather than demolish the past. Lenin seemed much, much smaller, perhaps shrunken in shame at his ignominious demotion.

MAYA JONES, AGE 17

My Room

Like a beach with a setting sun,
beige carpet as soft as Hawaiian sand between my toes,
a kaleidoscope of blue and white.

Paradise. A place where time pauses.
Relaxation and fun all in one.
My room brings a special feeling to my heart,
and I'm a happy girl when I get home from a long day.

My room is my best friend.
Cheers me up when I'm sad, or when I'm alone.
Warms me up when I am cold,
and keeps me safe when I sense harm.

I love my room
and it loves me back.

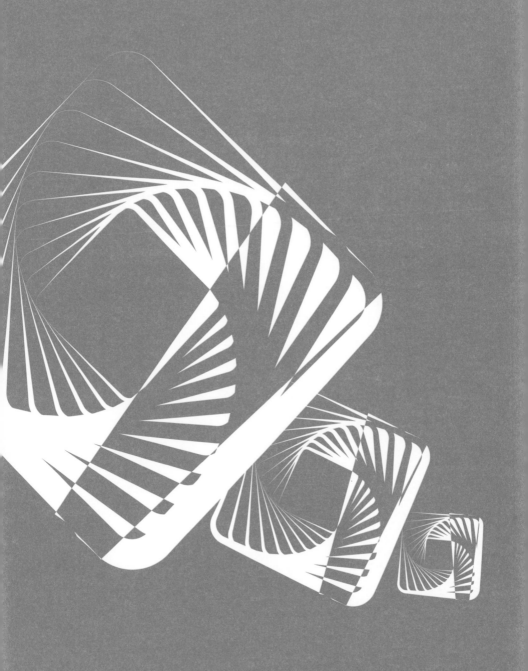

18
WOVEN FROM WHISPERS

Memory

Memories

Our memories
climb like rings of smoke
fading into the night sky.
Years swallowed whole in the firmament.
They dance in the ferocious midnight.
A shadow of mystique,
transformations
twist, curl and fade.
Minutes, Seconds, Moments.
Feet drag across the cobblestones.
They crowd the empty street,
searching
for hands outstretched,
fingers – shaking, old, and broken.
Time slips through our embrace,
slick with the harsh rain of remembrance.
They part with a final whisper,
but no recollection of what was said.

During a writers' workshop, we were asked to reflect on altars – those spaces in our homes that we reserve to honor the memory of loved ones.

Altar

Crisp white sheet
Cigar smoke
Silver coins around the giant pink-lipped conch
Fistfuls of sugar cane
A glass of water between
A coconut and Father's blue eye

Pasture:
shards of glass
Water buffalo tooth and sage bundles
Potato sack of locusts
A pistol or a Bible

Combat boots
Lipsticked collars and a photo of Joan
Dentures
A gilded watch near the bowl of infarcted arteries
12-fold flag
Wings

Or bottles of nail polish
A slice of red velvet cake
A bowl of wedding rings and humid licorice
Packs of Newport Slims
Lungs blistered with faith
collapsed to glory

This piece was inspired by all the people I care about and my close relationships in my family.

Grandpa's Visits

"Hey, Grandpa!" the little girl shouts as she steps into the garage.

He turns his head. "Elena! I would hug you, but I'm a little dirty from fixing the car." He wipes his forehead with his hand.

"It's okay, Grandpa. I'm really happy to see you again," she says.

"Me too, Mija. Come in and close the door." She sits on the floor.

Grandfather says, "Were you napping right now on Grandma's bed? I remember you always used to when I lived here."

Elena giggles. "How did you know?"

"You have those crusts in your eyes," Grandfather says, laughing. "You know who you remind me of? Your mother. She always had that after napping, too. I used to call her *Lagaña* – eye-crusts."

Elena starts to laugh but then stops. "She misses you, Grandpa. Why don't you go in and talk to her? Including Grandma."

"They wouldn't accept me, Elena," he says, his voice trembling. "I was so cruel to them."

"My mom won't tell me about it. I know it's something about money and how you wouldn't take it from her to pay for medicine..." says Elena.

"It was nothing, Mija. Your mother is fine without me and so is your grandma."

"I don't think you should keep sneaking in here, Grandpa! You'll get in trouble."

"Don't worry, Elena. This is the last time, I promise. It's because you still need me."

"Elena! Ven a comer! Come and eat!" shouts Elena's mother as she opens the door. "Elena what are you doing in there?"

"Talking to Grandpa."

Her mother's eyes widen. "Elena, Grandpa passed away months ago, remember?"

"I know, but sometimes I still find him here and we talk."

"What about?"

"You. You're so sad without him. He misses you too, Lagañas."

"Lagañas..." Her mother's eyes become glossy.

Memories should be expressed.

*I wrote this last summer while I was working on my novel.
It's written from the perspective of the lead female in my story.*

Summer Reflections

Hazy sunshine
hovers
like the scent of gardenia
as it embraces my hair

Hand in hand the
breeze carries your words
across the sea
glistening
bursts of light
beautiful, yet damaging

We first embraced here
in a time when children
still laughed
and innocence was
as abundant as the sand on
which we stood

Now the sea is my mirror
as deep and unpredictable
as the days before me

ERIN YARBROUGH, AGE 17

Nostalgia inspired this piece.

Three Feet

I feel like running through the sprinklers
In blue and pink water shoes
Feeling the warmth of sun-kissed water on my cheeks
Stomping around unevenly in puddles on bricks with sopping wet curls
Scream and shriek and laugh and love and shrink and melt
Revert back to innocence
Wipe my slate clean
Let the universe spin
While I lay sprawled
Under the waterfall
In the front yard of our house on Firebrand
And watch
The view
From
Three feet
Tall

Every time I have to figure out how to use parentheses I flash back to 4th grade (I still don't know how to use these things). My mentor was writing about a childhood memory, so I wrote one of my own.

Where the Sentence Ends

Lunch ends and the 4th graders migrate back to the classroom, some bouncing basketballs, others using their outside voice, clearly still feeling the effects of recess. You find your seat in between Calvin and Shant and listen to Miss Lee's directions: "Take out the narrative essays you've been working on and continue from yesterday."

Okay. No prob. Writing is your thing, Caroline, you'll be done in no time.

Suddenly a roadblock appears. How do you use parentheses again? Does the period go inside of the parentheses? You look to your left and right. Idiots on all sides. A boy would never know the answer to your question. You didn't want it to come to this, but it's time to consult Miss Lee.

Her response to the question is brief, "You put the period where the sentence ends."

So, where does the sentence end (or does it)?

I wrote a letter to my future daughter during a mentoring session.

On Clear Nights

Dear Daughter,

I will remember those green grasslands. The white and brown horses used instead of cars. In the mornings, roosters woke my cousins and me. We'd never be able to fall back to sleep, but I liked that. We'd get up and feed Michael, my grandmother's parrot. Then the flower lady would knock at our door. Some mornings, I picked the flowers from the back of her truck – reds, yellows, oranges and violets.

When the bells rang it was time for church. We'd get ready and head out the door into a cold December breeze. After church we'd devour chili candy until our tongues turned red. Later we'd get ready again, and, leaving behind hair straighteners, curling irons, high heels, scattered clothes and the sweet smells of hairspray mixed with Dolce & Gabbana perfume, we'd leave for the plaza where we ventured into the friendly streets.

On clear nights, trillions of stars covered the sky like a snow blanket. On those nights, sharing laughter and smiles, my cousins and I made memories that later, tucked into our beds, we'd re-live for hours. We'd talk about the guys who tried to talk to us and all the laughs we shared. Then we'd hear music. No surprise. It was the same teenage guys outside my grandma's house, blasting the speakers from their blue Volkswagen Beetle. We'd peek out the balcony, and they'd smile at us, and we would go down. But don't worry, they weren't strangers, they were my friends. This place was home, this is where I felt safe.

One day, I'll take you to the place where your mother made a lot of special memories, where you'll make your own. You'll fall in love with the lake, the grasslands, the horses, the people and especially the food.

Love,
Your Mother

This is a celebration of someone dear to me who I lost recently.

Pasquale

he was always so many things
sailor, cheerleader, trainer, warrior

mediator, charismatic leader, hard body, dreamer
idol, worshipped – father, brother, son

Philly boy, life of the party, disciplined even in revelry
"Drink your drink, woman" "Eat some meat"

beautiful smile, dancing eyes
perpetual student, filling in blanks

impatient, efficient, thoughts, emotions
strong but shrouded, vulnerable sweetness

after surviving awhile, an angel too soon
not forgotten, my lover, my SEAL

dream visitor, my protector,
soul fluttering, unconstrained by the world or the fire

on to different secret missions, other codes of grace
then, now, forever, there is never goodbye

a laugh I can still hear
a touch I can still feel
a funny name etched on my heart
until the end of time

I wrote this during a mentoring session. The prompt was to imagine that you have strings tied around your fingers, and write about the objects that are dangling from the strings.

Another World

A plane ticket dangles from my finger waiting patiently to take me to another world, a world full of surprises and emotions. The world that sets me free with the smell of dirt just after a rain and the screaming when one of the guys falls off the bull in the yard in front of my grandmother's house. The sound of dribbles and whistles when we play basketball just so the loser can pay for dinner.

The plane ticket, my ticket to explore this new world. The world my ancestors came from, where my parents made their childhood memories. Where I am myself. Where my kids will love to spend the summer as much as I do.

A plane ticket flying me to friends and family. Nights out. Spending money on Futbolitos and the rides that spin us time after time to see who gets the dizziest. Dancing until the moon dims and the first rays of sun paint the horizon blue. Taco stands, bread stands and ice cream stands inviting you for a taste.

The plane ticket that leads me to my dad, where I'm his little girl again. Where nothing else matters except our bond that once felt broken, but is now glued together and stronger. Where he relives his childhood with me, playing in the river, standing barefoot on the rocks. Splashing water where our shoes become boats, drifting with the current until we run after them. Where we watch people ride bulls while munching on chips and candy.

A plane ticket that is used for love. Love that unites my family as one. Love that connects friendships. Friendships that will last forever. Friendships that teach me about myself.

Don't think, just write.

Speak the truth.

Write what you feel.

My mom, Hazeline Covert, and I wrote this poem for my aunt's funeral.

So Long

"So long"…is what she said before hanging up the phone or leaving your home.

"So long"…is what she said after visiting during a joyous or sad occasion.

"So long"…is what she said from her hospital bed.

She never said goodbye. She always said…"So long."

So long

…my sister.

So long.

This is about forgiveness.

The Gardens at Monticello

An article about an upcoming book, written by the current manager of the gardens at Monticello, described how he paired historic knowledge with modern sustainability techniques. Immediately, I knew I had to get a copy of that book.

When I visited those gardens with you, many years ago, it was a mixed excursion. We didn't argue, but there were numerous silent episodes when either I was mad about how much you'd had to drink or you were sullen over some perceived rebuke about your driving. That day at Monticello, the air was very crisp. After a few cursory insights by the docent, I strolled around the small house and grounds and got more and more angry. Not at you, at Jefferson, but possibly it was really about you, too. Not long after that trip, we didn't speak anymore.

I figured I would just send the book, with no preamble. You'd recognize the extended hand. You ought to be the one reaching out, but I would. I'd order two copies, so we could look at it together and reminisce. It was not yet published, so I signed up for an email alert and waited.

Two years later, the copies finally arrived. I don't know what delayed publication, but I sent many emails to the author, to Yale University Press and to Monticello. Nobody ever wrote back. As I searched for the appropriate box, I imagined your reaction. Of course you would accept my gesture and return it in kind, pretending the intervening time apart did not matter. The day I was intending to mail the package, I got a call. You were gone. There was no need to send the book.

I sent it anyway, a kind of inexplicable gift, to be opened at your memorial service. My copy is still wrapped in cellophane. I haven't had the courage to thumb through it. I don't have a garden. I'm still back and forth in my admiration and disdain for Jefferson, but I'm certain I shouldn't have waited.

There is no such thing
as a typical day in
a writer's life.

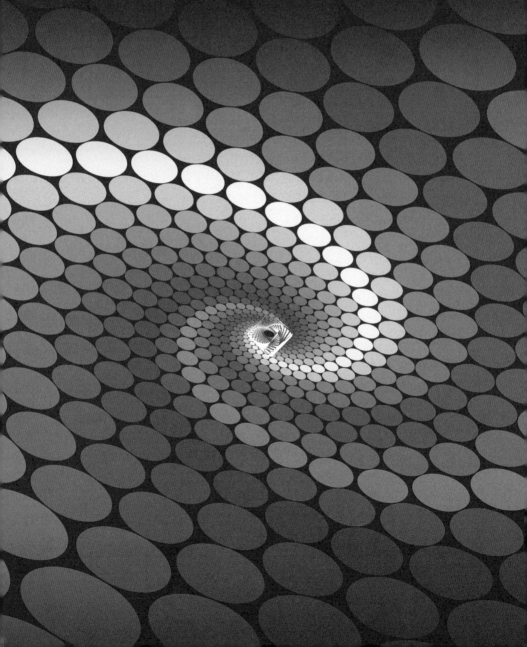

KAELYN LUSTIG, AGE 14

I wrote this at a WriteGirl workshop. We were writing about ancestors. This reminded me of when my mom and I were cleaning out the linen closet and found a handkerchief that my great-grandmother had made.

Memories Covered in Dust

In the bottom of a linen closet,
surrounded by cloth,
a handmade handkerchief quivers.

Lace covered in dust,
simple beauty obscured by darkness,
a memory not remembered.

But light reappears, slicing through stale air.
The lace is held again by new hands.
This generation pats away the dust.

The memory is re-remembered,
the simple beauty seen.
It has been found.

All You Need to Do Is Dream

Making Sense of Memories

Use Different Words

Where Am I?

Do Unto Others

Outside Influences

Conceptual Definition

Inside Out

The Snowball

Alternate Viewpoints

Bonsai

Idiom-Inspired

Grand Letters and Bold Speeches

19
GET LOST

Writing Experiments

OUTSIDE INFLUENCES

The world around you is filled with sights and sounds to inspire your writing. Museums and hiking trails are obvious sources of inspiration, but don't miss out on the intrigue that menus and billboards can provide.

Stop and look around you: Choose an individual item to be your inspiration. Study the item to discover every detail, and consider what makes it interesting to you. Write a short piece of fiction or a poem that includes this item as a key component, or incorporate some words and phrases from your description of the item in your writing.

NOW TRY THIS:

Listen to the conversations around you — write down a few phrases that stand out. Incorporate one or more lines of this "found language" into your composition.

MIRIAM SACHS, AGE 15

Ghost Bird

I lost a staring contest with the bronze ghost bird at the Autry.
It had no pupils in its eyes, no eyelids for blinking.

Above its beak, the turkey wore a flimsy rhinoceros horn,
a forgotten flap of skin, sore and exposed.

Its neck, skinnier than I'll ever be, but the body
– broad and beautiful like a burnt mountain cut out of wood or stone.

"What a great centerpiece for Thanksgiving,"
said a small Asian lady with zebra pants and a bob.

Your readers have the biggest and smallest hold over you.

WHERE AM I?

Imagine yourself in an unexpected location, and explore your thoughts and feelings about being there. You can be literal in describing your surroundings and how you got there, or you can consider how the place might be a metaphor for something else. Almost any place can inspire a great piece of writing and create a powerful metaphor to access a unique point of view.

Here's a list of places and themes to inspire just a few of the ways you might use a location as a metaphor:

> In a doorway (new beginnings, departures)
> Watching a sunrise (gaining strength, getting warmed up, getting ready for something)
> On a mountain (looking over everything, seeing the entirety of something)
> In jail (trapped, confined, locked in)
> At the edge of a cliff (in a state of suspense or on the brink of something)

NOW TRY THIS:

Add a question mark somewhere in your piece, or turn a statement into a question.

Trapped

I am in jail.
Locked in a cage, with no way to escape.
I am a prisoner.
Secured in a box by society.
But I am not giving up.
Give me the keys. I want out.

Does the key even exist?

Let me go. I am done being your songbird.
Let me fly free.
I am so much more than you're letting me be.

Release me, you won't be sorry.
I deserve the chance to show you what I can do.
I need to show you what I am.

CONCEPTUAL DEFINITION

A word can mean so much more than its literal definition in the dictionary.
What do the ideas below mean to you? Pick one and start writing. Be specific.
Draw from your own experiences of the word. Use imagery and metaphor.
Use all your senses – what does this idea look, smell, taste, feel, sound like?
Turn the idea and your words into a poem, a song or a story.

> Peace
> Friendship
> Exhaustion
> Inspiration
> Mornings

NOW TRY THIS:

Read your piece aloud. Feel the rhythm. Find
places where repetition might emphasize the
mood or idea you are trying to convey.

NOW TRY THIS TOO:

For poetry, read the ends of all of your lines,
and see if the last words or phrases on each
line are the ones that are the most visual and
evocative. For example, "the," "and," "to," or "for,"
have less impact than words like, "melody," "eyelid,"
"in-between" and "plum sky," as you can see in the
poem on the following page by Amanda Gorman

AMANDA GORMAN, AGE 14

Poetry Is

Poetry is your voice when you don't have one
Poetry is a song when there is no melody
It is in the sea glass an old woman hangs above her porch
It is who you are when you don't know

Don't say poetry, because it is not what it is at all
It is the mind, the soul, the spirit, when they can't be contained
Like the blazing sun against a plum sky
Permanently imprinted behind her eyes
Say poetry, because it is what it is

Poetry is the tear you didn't want to perch on your eyelid
Poetry is the pain that brings you relief
It is the waves in the ocean, the surface clear as glass
But the currents underneath hectic as your soul
Whisper Poetry, when it can't be understood
Love those who refuse things that can't be comprehended

It is the silver sun and the yellow moon
It is the black light and the bright dark
And when you are done, you will see poetry is nothing
At all and anything you can think of
For it is everything in-between

GRAND LETTERS AND BOLD SPEECHES

Words matter. They can inspire people, influence politics, introduce new ideas and even change the world. Write a letter or speech to a specific group of people, like all the artists, or teachers or women of the world. What does this group need to hear from you, right now?

Here are a few more audiences to get you started:

> World Leaders
> Chefs
> Writers
> Soldiers
> Comedians
> Shoemakers

NOW TRY THIS:

Go back to the letter or speech you just wrote. How can you make it stronger? Try incorporating questions that will make you audience think. For example, "Shoemakers of the world, why don't you make shoes that last longer than one year?" "World Leaders, if you own parts of the ocean, don't you have to take care of it?"

ANGELLE KING, AGE 15

Dear Women

We are powerful. In society, people constantly say, "It's a man's world," but it's not just that. It's our world, too!

Women have power and just as much potential for greatness. We, as women, can achieve whatever our hearts desire. We are equal, capable and strong. We can overcome and accomplish anything through perseverance and determination. We must never give up or let anyone or anything get in the way.

We will dream big. We will stand. We are women!

Plan out the plot before writing. It keeps you from going nowhere midway through the story.

IDIOM-INSPIRED

Idioms are phrases that create a metaphor beyond the literal
meaning of the words. Use one of these idioms as a jumping off
point to tell a story from your own life. Feel free to play with the
idiom instead of using it verbatim.

> The grass is always greener
> Piece of cake
> Penny for your thoughts
> When pigs fly
> Break a leg
> Let the cat out of the bag

NOW TRY THIS:

Pick a situation or moment from your
story and write the dialogue for it. How
would the conversation go? Let us hear
their voices.

EMILY BURTON, AGE 15

Penny for Her Thoughts

I never knew my grandmother Penny. She was a phoenix raised from the ashes, an unseen angel that lit the fire in my mother's eyes. Born Gertrude, she redefined herself early on. My mother spoke of her with sadness and a quiet triumph. She spoke of a woman beaten down so that her own mind betrayed her as her stepmother and first husband had.

When Penny was young, she wore her long, dark hair in braids that the boys at school would dip in inkwells. Out of jealousy or spite, Penny's stepmother came to her bedroom as she was sleeping one night. Penny woke up the next morning with only one braid, and would have worn it proudly if she'd had her way.

When Penny was old, no one needed to ask for her thoughts. When angry, she spoke only to the white lamp on the end table, yelling just as loud as she could manage. If the neighbors couldn't hear her complaining about my grandfather to her lamp, she had already turned them deaf.

When my mother was young, it was Penny who gave her the strength to choose her own path. Now, when my body feels beaten and my mind betrays me, it is Penny I think of, and I look to the flickering lamp on the end table.

ALTERNATE VIEWPOINTS

Imagine you are experiencing the world from a different point of
view, such as that of another person, an animal or, in the case of
the poem on the following page, a baby. Try to create a situation
and imagine how your character would react. It can be something
extraordinary or an everyday event. What do you hear and see? How
do you feel? How do people react to you? What new perspective do
you gain by looking at the world through someone else's eyes? Do
you see the world at knee-level, like a dog or a cat, or do you see
everything, like a fly-on-the-wall?

Pretend that you are:

> Invisible
> Much older or younger than yourself
> A bird flying overhead
> A person from another time in history
> A lost pet trying to get back home
> An extra in an adventure movie

NOW TRY THIS:

*Describe your character's experience
through all of the five senses (sight,
smell, taste, touch and sound). Does
your character have a sixth sense?*

Car Seat

Dum, dum, dum, dum
My head hits the car.
The seat on my back is snug,
curving to the shape of my back.

The seatbelt is buckled,
across my tired body.
I lean back and scream.
I want to be free.

The leather car seat
squeaks as I tighten
my grip on it.
He says:
Fine. Be free, but I will be behind you.

My knuckles turn pink again,
As the blood rushes back to my fingers.
The seat slowly slips away from my fingers
I am a free babe.
I sigh with relief
I can sing,
fly,
scream.

I am a free babe.
Thank you, car seat, for having my back.

MAKING SENSE OF MEMORIES

Have you ever noticed that the scent, taste or feel of something can remind you of something else – a person you haven't seen for a long time, or a place you used to go? How about when you hear a song, or see an old movie? The next time something you feel, taste, smell, see or hear triggers a memory, write down everything you can remember.

Here are some phrases to get you started:

> Whenever I taste cinnamon, I think of...
> That song reminds me of the time I...
> The smell of rain reminds me of...
> When I see this sweater I think of...
> The feel of grass under my feet makes me remember when...

NOW TRY THIS:

Change the tense of your piece to put it in the present, as if it's all happening right now. Or, if you wrote in the present, try setting it in the future. See how time affects the tone of your writing.

Watermelon

The salty fresh smell
Memories rushing
Gushing like a tsunami
Childhood
Summer nights
Spinning ferris wheel lights
Days at the beach
Bike riding with my dad
That salty fresh smell
Easter in the park
Yellows, purples, pinks,
Family evenings
Grandpa's lectures
Mom's warm hands
Statements of love

ALL YOU NEED TO DO IS DREAM

Dreams can inspire stories. Think about the last dream you had, or take a few notes the next time someone tells you about a dream they had. Flesh out the details, change a few along the way, let one idea lead to another. Don't stop writing until you have the beginning of a song, story or poem.

Tip: Keep a dream journal next to your bed. Don't forget the pen!

NOW TRY THIS:

Use specific names of things. A street name, the brand of cookie your character is eating or the type of tree they are climbing will bring your story to life and make it more visual.

AUNYE SCOTT-ANDERSON, AGE 17

Not Like Other Girls

I could feel it, hot and blossoming from my knee. Blood spilled down my leg as I ran alongside Doja down to the shadowed area beneath the bridge. The sound of sirens grew closer, blaring threats of incarceration that she and I no longer cringed at. We lay our bodies flat along the damp moss and overgrown grass that sprouted at the base of the bridge. The ground vibrated beneath our prostrated bodies, the blood from my cut smeared across my leg becoming one with the earth.

The police gave up much too quickly and soon retreated when their flashlights failed to spot the weeping willow ponytail that sprouted my midnight black locks. Doja sprang up first, the denim backpack she carried jangled with the remains of our spray paint cans and pens. She released an exasperated laugh and helped me to my feet. I looked down to examine my cut – I didn't quite make it smoothly over the wire gate of the recently closed down elementary school.

WRITING EXPERIMENTS

THE SNOWBALL

Like a snowball that gets bigger as it rolls down a hill, this experiment allows you to start with something simple, then expand it and use the momentum to create a more complex and specific image or idea.

Start with a simple phrase or sentence and write it down. Next, create a simile to replace it. Then, turn the simile into a metaphor. Now, add specific details that incorporate two or more of the five senses (sight, sound, touch, smell, taste). Finally, include additional details that reveal more of Who?, What?, When?, Where?, Why? and How?.

NOW TRY THIS:

Go back to one of the previous writing experiments and apply one or more of these techniques to one of your sentences or phrases.

Mermaid

Starting sentence:
She walked in.

Simile:
She waddled like a mermaid out of water.

Metaphor:
She was a mermaid out of water.

Sensory:
A mermaid out of water, her marshmallow eyes were a pale shade of ocean blue and she smelled like sea salt, too.

Who, What, When, Where, Why or *How:*
A mermaid out of Detroit River water, Maggie's marshmallow eyes were a pale shade of Santa Monica ocean blue and she smelled like Baltic Sea salt, too.

MORE WRITING EXPERIMENTS MORE GENRES

FICTION

Pick a profession – taxidermist, pancake flipper, mortician, ice sculptor, etc. – and write a first-person account of an unusual day at work.

MIX IT UP:

Turn this story into a news article. Start with a catchy headline.

....

JOURNALISM

Interview someone you admire and create a "profile": tell us about their goals, their achievements, their favorite foods, what makes them smile. Try to find out something unexpected about this extraordinary person.

SWITCH GENRES:

Turn your profile into a story song – Google "Bad, Bad Leroy Brown" for an example!

....

MEMOIR

Write about a day you received a gift that meant a lot to you. Use as much detail as possible. What did it look like? How heavy was it? Did it have a particular smell? Who gave it you? Why? Why was it special to you?

KEEP GOING:

Let your memory wander...let one memory lead to the next. Free write about whatever comes to mind when you think about this gift, person or event.

SONGWRITING

Write a song to celebrate a season. What do you love to do during this season? What frustrates you about it? Pick a rhyme scheme (ABAB, AABB, etc.) and write one or two verses and a chorus as a tribute to this time of year.

GRAB ANY SCRAP OF PAPER:

Play with writing "near rhymes" instead of the most obvious rhyming words. Make a word cloud of all the words you can think of that rhyme, or nearly rhyme, with the first word you've chosen. "Away, behave, sway, decay, brave..."

....

POETRY

Ever notice how many fancy names there are for blue? Sky, turquoise, navy, azure, peacock... pick a color and write as many different names for that color as you can think of. Online shopping sites or catalogs are a good source for descriptive names. Write a poem about the color orange, that never uses the word "orange."

GET FIRED UP:

Choose an emotion (angry, joyful, confused, bored, etc.) and revise your piece to convey that specific feeling.

CHARACTER DEVELOPMENT

Your character has a secret! Write a confessional monologue in which he or she tells this secret to someone he/she has never met before.

TELL US MORE:

Write the conversation between your character and someone else involved in the secret.

DIALOGUE

Write a scene in which two people are arguing; person A is about to go somewhere, and person B tries to stop him/her. How and why?

NOW TRY THIS:

Add two or three physical actions as stage direction to show the reader what your characters are doing, like (slams the door) or (waves goodbye).

Don't be afraid of where your inspiration stems from. It doesn't matter if it's from a dream, while taking a test or even in the shower – let it take you where it wants to go.

YOU'RE NOT DONE YET! EDITING EXPERIMENTS

Take a first draft and turn it into a polished piece by trying one of these experiments... or all of them!

"BONSAI"

Similar to the art of bonsai, you can trim or prune your poem so that only the most beautiful parts remain. With your first draft, remove as many of the helper words as you can. When you take away words such as *the*, *of*, *and*, *like*, *there*, *is*, etc., the words that are left behind become more important.

Here's an example:

BEFORE
The submerged rays of sun were split
like spun glass,
and they moved themselves
into the crevices of the ocean.

AFTER
The sun's submerged rays, split.
Spun glass moved
into the ocean's crevices.

USE DIFFERENT WORDS

Go through your piece and underline or circle repeated words –
specifically adjectives and nouns – not words like *and* or *the*. Come
up with new words or phrases to replace the duplicates.

....

INSIDE OUT

List the emotional words in your piece (i.e. hurt, smiling, confused)
and create a simile, metaphor or image for each emotion. Choose at
least one of the images and insert it into your piece.

....

DO UNTO OTHERS

Editing another person's work is good practice for calling up your inner-
editor. Use the Internet to find a short piece of poetry or prose and pretend
you have been asked to step in as Editor and make it stronger. Once you're
done, reflect on the approaches you took and then try to apply the same
level of objectivity to your own unedited work.

The best views are written.

This is WriteGirl

Never underestimate the power of a girl and her pen.

"My experience
has been **excellent,**
fun, **exciting,** inspiring,
beautiful and **delicious."**

– WriteGirl mentee

WriteGirl is a creative writing and mentoring organization for teen girls. Founded in 2001, with just 30 girls and 30 volunteers, WriteGirl currently serves more than 300 teen girls throughout Los Angeles County with 150 volunteers.

Girls from more than 75 schools participate in the Core Mentoring Program where WriteGirl pairs teen girls with professional women writers for one-on-one mentoring, workshops, public readings and publication in award-winning, nationally distributed anthologies. WriteGirl also provides individual college and financial aid guidance to every participant.

WriteGirl works!

For the twelfth year in a row, WriteGirl has successfully guided 100% of the seniors in its Core Mentoring Program to not only graduate from high school but also enroll in college, with many obtaining full or partial scholarships.

WriteGirl also brings weekly creative writing workshops to critically at-risk teen girls through its innovative In-Schools Program. Launched in 2004, the WriteGirl In-Schools Program currently serves four Los Angeles County Office of Education schools in the communities of Lawndale, Azusa, South Los Angeles and Santa Clarita. Students at three of these schools are pregnant or parenting teens, foster youths, on probation, have been assigned social workers or are unable to return to their home schools due to any number of issues. The fourth school is the Road to Success Academy in Santa Clarita at Camp Scott and Camp Scudder, which are adjacent juvenile detention facilities.

Girls who participate in WriteGirl develop vital communication skills, self-confidence, critical thinking skills, deeper academic engagement and enhanced creativity for a lifetime of increased opportunities.

"I learned that **my thoughts** and ideas do matter."
– WriteGirl mentee

DISCOVERY

"I love all the good **creative** energy!"
– WriteGirl mentee

Alumnae Highlights

Alma Castrejon, a UC Riverside and Cal State Long Beach graduate, works for the UCLA Labor Center, focusing on immigrant rights and outreach.

Jeanine Daniels, a Pitzer College graduate, is a writer and producer of the acclaimed web series, *The Couple,* and is working on her first feature film.

Ariel Edwards-Levy, a USC graduate, is a political journalist with the *Huffington Post* in Washington, D.C.

Glenda Garcia, a Dickinson College graduate, is a WriteGirl staff member focusing on membership, after returning from a year as a Fulbright Scholar in Thailand.

Jennifer Gottesfield, a UCLA graduate, is working on public health initiatives and mentoring youth in Malawi.

Nadine Levyfield, a UC Berkeley graduate, recently completed a year-long national fellowship with Hillel in Washington, D.C., and is working in philanthropy in Los Angeles.

Perla Melendez, a UC Santa Barbara graduate, is a teacher at the Heads Up program.

Corrie Siegel, a Bard College graduate, is an education manager at the Fowler Museum in Los Angeles.

Jennifer Swann, an Art Institute of Chicago graduate, is a writer for the *Los Angeles Weekly*.

Lovely Umayam, a Reed College graduate, is a fellow with the U.S. Department of Energy, focusing on nuclear nonproliferation.

WriteGirl alumnae Majah Carberry and Victoria Tsou, back at a WriteGirl workshop to talk to the high school WriteGirls about what college is like.

Associate Director Allison Deegan with her mentee and WriteGirl alumna, Lovely Umayam.

*Remarks by WriteGirl alumna
Glenda Garcia given at the
Bold Ink Awards November 5, 2012*

In high school, I realized there was nowhere to go for a girl like me —
a Latina with a lot of angst, idealistic dreams and enormous ideas
of how things should be in a fair world. I was so fortunate to find
WriteGirl, an organization that was not only invested in my success,
but also genuinely cared about what I had to say.

WriteGirl provides a safe space for young women to establish their
voices as writers, activists, artists and much more. WriteGirl is a
stepping-stone to marvelous opportunities.

During college application season, my WriteGirl mentor nominated
me for the full-tuition Posse Foundation scholarship. In 2005, I
commenced my time at Dickinson College as a Posse Scholar. This
allowed me to intern in our nation's capital and travel to India and
Venezuela. I graduated Magna Cum Laude from Dickinson College
with a degree in Women's and Gender Studies. I joined AmeriCorps
VISTA as an after school coordinator and teacher for an
underprivileged community in Arizona. My time with WriteGirl
helped me understand that learning does not end in the classroom.
It flows out into community centers, coffee shops, bookstores,
libraries and especially mentoring programs.

I recently completed my term as a Fulbright grantee in Thailand.
My journey there began at my first WriteGirl workshop in 2002. As
a low-income Latina from a single-parent household, I know that I
would not be the woman I am without WriteGirl's guidance and
support. WriteGirl allowed me to enhance my writing and speaking
skills through one-on-one mentoring and public readings.

I was allowed to share my opinions with professional women writers without the limitations of a school bell or an impatient schoolteacher. WriteGirl is a family that I turn to for inspiration, support and motivation.

I am honored to stand here tonight sharing my love for a group of women that are truly changing the world one girl at a time.

As we say in Thailand, *Sawaadee Ka!*

– Glenda Garcia, WriteGirl alumna

WriteGirl alumna Glenda Garcia, speaking at the 2012 WriteGirl Bold Ink Awards.

"I really enjoy the positive energy dedicated to finding a girl's voice."

— WriteGirl Volunteer

Mentoring pairs work together for a day, a project or all through high school.

"I got positive feedback, which I really liked because I've always been afraid of what people will say."

— WriteGirl Mentee

WriteGirl mentor and mentee.

Mentoring

WriteGirl matches professional women writers with teen girls for one-on-one mentoring and creative writing. Every week, mentoring pairs write at coffee shops, libraries, museums or other creative locations. They write, reflect and inspire each other. WriteGirl screens, selects and trains women writers to prepare them to be effective writing mentors, with mentor advisors providing support and help throughout the year. Each month, 150 women writers contribute 2,000 volunteer hours as workshop leaders and volunteers.

Guest songwriter Holly Palmer gives expert advice to a WriteGirl at a workshop at Disney Concert Hall.

"WriteGirl is great because my mentor always has time to give me honest feedback on my work. It's encouraging to know that someone other than my mom believes that I can succeed as a professional writer."

– WriteGirl Mentee

Workshops

WriteGirl workshops offer our membership the opportunity to explore new writing genres in a fun, creative and highly interactive environment. Nearly every month as many as 150 women and girls gather to experiment with poetry, songwriting, monologue and dialogue, fiction, non-fiction or journalism. Workshops feature experiential and self-paced learning activities, emphasize a collaborative approach involving mentors and mentees learning from each other, and include special guests who provide girls with their insights from the world of professional writing.

Writing activities happen all over the room — not just sitting at tables!

WriteGirls find inspiration by writing in beautiful spaces.

Workshops Manager Kirsten Giles keeps hundreds of people energized and excited all day!

"I like the creative juices that this workshop squeezed out of me."
– WriteGirl Mentee

"This morning I didn't even think I could write a song, but by the end of the day I was listening to my own lyrics being sung. Amazing!"
– WriteGirl Mentee

Spinning the wheel gives WriteGirls themes, challenges or perhaps just a new word.

Special Guests

Communications & Journalism:

Karen Grigsby Bates
Alexandra Berzon
Erica Blodgett
Dalina Castellanos
Jia-Riu Cook
Mona Gable
Francesca James
Alexandra Zavis

Creative Nonfiction and Memoir:

Amy Friedman
Diane Glancy
Andrea Rogers

Fiction:

Katie Alender
Cecil Castelluci
Francesca Lia Block

Poetry:

Xochitl-Julisa Bermejo
Carol Cellucci
Jen Hofer
Terry Wolverton

Performance Workshops:

Natalie Patterson
Nikki Vescovi
Leah Yananton

Literary Panel at Mentor Retreat:

Judy Carter
Kim Dower
Amy Friedman

Career Panel for Summer Interns:

Maria del Pilar O'Cadiz
Tabby Biddle
Alexandra Armstrong
Alex Schaffert-Callaghan
Juliet Flores
Jennifer Rustigian

Author Cecil Castelluci leads a quick workshop at the Los Angeles Central Library, prior to the *No Character Limit* Book Launch.

Journalist Elizabeth Espinosa gives career and writing advice at the *Los Angeles Times* Festival of Books.

Novelist Francesca Lia Block shares secrets at the Petersen Automotive Museum.

Songwriting:

Michelle Bell
Danielle Brisebois
Deanna DellaCiopa
Laurie Geltman
Natalie Nicole Gilbert
Adrianne Gonzales
Kari Kimmel
Holly Knight
Libby Lavella
Michelle Lewis
Clare Means
Lisa Nemzo
Holly Palmer
Simone Porter
Lindy Robbins
Janet Robin
Heidi Rojas
Celeste Scalone
Renee Stahl
Judy Stakee
Jonelle Vette

Character & Dialogue:

Script Doctors:
Jane Anderson
Stephanie Carrie
Susan Dickes
Toni Graphia
Jennifer Hoppe
Meg Jackson
Andrea King
Elizabeth Kruger
Clare Sera

Actors:
Keiko Agena
Wes Anderhold
Jessica Andres
Tracy Burns
Ron Butler
Julia Cho
Ashley Clements
Aasha Davis
Amanda Detmer
Dan Gauthier
Janice Lee
Hannah Marks
Suzy Nakamura
Mike Rock
Ryan Smith
Laura Spencer
Trevor St. John
Mary Kate Wiles

Special Events:

Ben Allen
Aasha Davis
Dr. Arturo Delgado
Elizabeth Espinosa
Edi Gathegi
Toni Graphia
Pamela Guest
Tahereh Mafi
Chris Messina
Ransom Riggs
Elizabeth Sarnoff
Clare Sera
Trevor St. John
Marcia Wallace
Robin Weigert

Songwriter Janet Robin improvises melodies for lyrics written by the WriteGirl teens at the Songwriting Workshop at Walt Disney Concert Hall.

WriteGirl teens read their work at public events all over Los Angeles. Our girls learn that telling their stories in front of a live audience is fun, empowering and inspiring.

Public Readings

To celebrate the book launch of WriteGirl's 11th anthology *No Character Limit: Truth & Fiction from WriteGirl*, the girls shared their poetry and prose in front of nearly 200 people at the **Los Angeles Central Library**. The event was followed by a dessert reception and plenty of accolades.

WriteGirl readings take place at different venues, including the **West Hollywood Book Fair, the** *Los Angeles Times* **Festival of Books, Skylight Books** and **the Writers Guild of America Theater.**

"When people read the book they come up to me and say, 'Hi, I saw your work.' It feels really good."
– WriteGirl Mentee

<<<<<<<<<<<<<<<<

"It's empowering to hear other girls speak and to see that it's possible to become a writer."
– WriteGirl Mentee

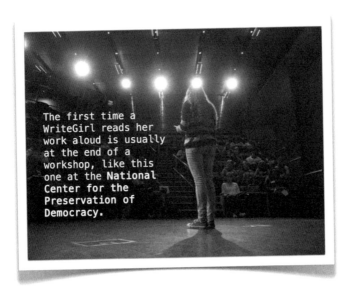

The first time a WriteGirl reads her work aloud is usually at the end of a workshop, like this one at the **National Center for the Preservation of Democracy.**

"I loved listening to my shy daughter read on stage."
– WriteGirl Parent

WriteGirl wraps up the year with a reading where all the girls get a copy of the anthology with their work.

Readings are an opportunity to share brand new work, as well as writing that has been published in one of the annual anthologies.

Family, friends and strangers make up the audience at our public readings.

Interns
learn
valuable
skills and
develop
their
resumes.

Internships
give girls a
chance to meet
people who
share their
interests and
ambition.

"WriteGirl has given me the foundation and confidence I needed to pursue other jobs and internships. I was able to grow so much from interning at WriteGirl because I was never stuck doing one task. I'm proud and feel so accomplished to have been an intern at WriteGirl!"

— WriteGirl Intern

"I see this as preparation for the future."

— WriteGirl Intern

Bold Futures

WriteGirl develops leaders. The WriteGirl Bold Futures Program weaves together a full slate of college and job preparedness skill building, as well as leadership development, to truly give young women the tools, community, confidence and tenacious communication skills they need to thrive in college, the workplace and in life. The Bold Futures Program offers intensive opportunities for high school seniors and college students to participate on planning committees, at special events and as interns in the WriteGirl office.

WriteGirl holds a career workshop to help interns better understand the working world.

"I literally learned something new every day. Whether it was specific to WriteGirl, the nonprofit world, writing or just life in general I never left the office without new knowledge. I was challenged by the internship [which] allowed me to notice my progress and measure my success."

— WriteGirl Intern

Publications

Since 2001, WriteGirl Publications has been producing award-winning anthologies that showcase the bold voices and imaginative insights of women and girls. Unique in both design and content, WriteGirl anthologies present a wide range of personal stories, poetry, essays, scenes and lyrics. WriteGirl inspires readers to find their own creative voices through innovative writing experiments and writing tips from both teens and their mentors.

Twelve anthologies from WriteGirl showcase the work of over 1,000 women and girls. Selections range from serious to whimsical, personal to political, and heartrending to uplifting.

WriteGirl anthologies have collectively won 55 national and international book awards!

ForeWord Reviews, School Library Journal, Kirkus, Los Angeles Times Book Review, The Writer Magazine and *VOYA* have all raved about WriteGirl books.

Pens on Fire, WriteGirl's educator's guide, offers over 200 inspiring writing experiments for teens and adults. Through the innovative use of props, movement, art, music, textures, scents and even flavors, *Pens on Fire* offers step—by—step creative writing curricula for teachers and youth leaders.

"The creative process is clearly cathartic for the teens and mentors, acting both as an outlet and as a tool to help them make better sense of the world around them. Adolescents reading this anthology will recognize themselves in the words."
— *School Library Journal*

"...girls and their mentors...explore universal feelings about friendship, family and adolescence."
— *Ms. Magazine* "Great reads"

Order WriteGirl books from www.WriteGirl.org,
www.Amazon.com or bookstores nationwide.

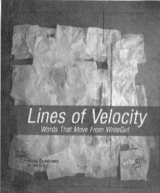

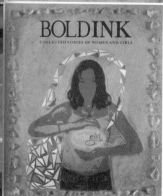

Support WriteGirl. Buy Our Anthologies!
www.writegirl.org
ALL PROCEEDS BENEFIT WRITEGIRL PROGRAMS

Bold Ink Awards

The annual WriteGirl Bold Ink Awards were created to honor the women who inspire our girls, our mentors and audiences around the world. We seek out storytellers whose voices move us. Their genres represent the breadth of our own membership and their achievements mark the degree of excellence we all strive for. They write in **Bold Ink.**

The 6th Annual Bold Ink Awards evening was held at the Eli and Edythe Broad Stage in Santa Monica. Honorees shared inside stories of writing challenges and successes, and WriteGirl alumna Glenda Garcia spoke about her journey from mentee to Fulbright scholar.

Past Bold Ink Award Honorees:

Diablo Cody
Wanda Coleman
Liz Craft
Jennifer Crittenden
Kara DioGuardi
Savannah Dooley
Sarah Fain
Janet Fitch
Carol Flint
Naomi Foner
Winnie Holzman
Callie Khouri
Gigi Levangie
Sandra Tsing Loh

Suzanne Lummis
Aline Brosh McKenna
Nancy Meyers
Patt Morrison
Carol Muske-Dukes
Sonia Nazario
Gina Prince-
    Bythewood
Lynda Resnick
Elizabeth Sarnoff
Carolyn See
Patricia Seyburn
Marisa Silver
Sarah Silverman
Mona Simpson
Jill Soloway
Robin Swicord
Nia Vardalos
Diane Warren

"This is an amazing honor."

— Margaret Stohl,
Bold Ink Awards Honoree

"Everybody is told
at some point that
they're not good
enough. When you
keep doing your
work, you win."

— Zoe Kazan, Bold Ink
Awards Honoree

Bold Ink awardees Lisa Cholodenko, Kami Garcia,
Margaret Stohl and Melissa Rosenberg.

"I think the honorees were
sincerely awed by
WriteGirl, which
translated to those in the
audience as absolutely
inspirational. I loved
meeting Glenda, the young
Fulbright scholar who
spoke. I think she really
brought home the work
that WriteGirl does."

— Bold Ink Awards guest

Actor/screenwriter
Zoe Kazan accepts
her award.

"It was an elegant
soiree ensnared
with femme
fatale... an
incredible
evening that
left attendees
inspired and
honored the
strides that
women are
making as
writers."

— Erica Nusgart,
Socialitelife.com

Actor Edi Gathegi
presented the
Bold Ink Award
to *Twilight*
series
screenwriter
Melissa
Rosenberg.

Awards for WriteGirl

2013	Women Making a Difference Award, *Los Angeles Business Journal*, Finalist
2013	SHero Award for Allison Deegan, WriteGirl Associate Director
2012	Albert R. Rodriguez Civic Legacy Award
2011	President's National Youth, Arts and Humanities Program Awards, Finalist
2011	Women Making a Difference Award, *Los Angeles Business Journal*, Finalist
2010-11	California Nonprofit of the Year by Governor Arnold Schwarzenegger and Maria Shriver
2010	HUMANITAS Philanthropy Prize for Work Empowering Writers
2010	Annenberg Alchemy Leadership Community Champion
2010	Ruby Award: Women Helping Women, Soroptimist International
2009	CA Governor and First Lady's Medal for Service, Finalist, Nonprofit Leader
2009	Springfield College School of Human Services Community Hero Award
2008	President's Volunteer Call to Service Award
2008	Community Woman of Achievement, Business & Professional Women Hollywood
2008	Women Making a Difference Award, *Los Angeles Business Journal*, Finalist
2007	Certificate of Appreciation, Los Angeles Mayor Antonio Villaraigosa
2006	Making a Difference for Women Award, Soroptimist International
2006	Certificate of Achievement, Los Angeles Mayor Antonio Villaraigosa
2006	Governor Arnold Schwarzenegger Commendation Letter
2006	Senator Gilbert Cedillo, 2nd District of CA, Commendation
2006	Gloria Molina, Supervisor, 1st District of California, Commendation
2006	Fabian Núñez, Speaker of the Assembly, Certification of Recognition
2006	Congressman Ed Reyes, 1st District of Los Angeles, Commendation
2005	Certificate of Appreciation, Los Angeles Mayor Antonio Villaraigosa
2004	President's Volunteer Call to Service Award

Praise for WriteGirl

"I love watching the girls when **they can't stop writing.** They're inspiring."
— WriteGirl Volunteer

"WriteGirl is one of **the best things that has ever happened** to me. Every year is something new and **it always gets better.**"
— WriteGirl Mentee

"I like being with other people who care about **giving back** to girls in the literary world."
— WriteGirl Volunteer

"I love the **fearlessness** of all the people that shared their writing."
— Special Guest

"It is astonishing how brave a woman is alone, but how **strong women are together.**"
— Special Guest

"I love the idea of **a door opening** to a girl's heart and brain."
— Mentor

"This was such a positive environment. I feel better after coming here."
— WriteGirl Mentee

"Hearing other girls' writing has increased her confidence in her own written expression."
— WriteGirl Parent

You Know You're a WriteGirl When...

You just feel like you need to write first thing in the morning.

You share your ideas and feelings.

You write 24/7.

You write from the heart.

You write a novel to answer a one word question for math class.

You write.

You keep writing.

You want to be a novelist, screenwriter, songwriter and journalist all at the same time.

You come up with poems in bed when you can't sleep.

You wake up early on a WriteGirl workshop morning wondering what's for lunch!

Your pen never stops moving!

You can relax and express yourself like there's no tomorrow.

You notice aspects of life that others don't.

You let your ideas flow.

You create!

– group poem by WriteGirl mentees

WriteGirl Works

WRITEGIRL LEADERSHIP:

Executive Director
Keren Taylor

Associate Director
Allison Deegan

Workshops Manager
Kirsten Giles

Administrative Assistant
Anna Mkhikian

Operations Coordinator
Glenda Garcia

In-Schools Program Manager
Brande Jackson

Grants Associate
Cindy Collins

Silent Auction Coordinator
Retta Putignano

Publications Coordinator
Rachel Fain

Event Assistants
Leslie Awender
Natalie Cohen
Tammy Connors
Christina Diaz
Jessica Freedman
Whitney Heleker
Lindsay Mendoza
Jamie Shaw

Intern Supervisor and Bold Futures Support
Naomi Buckley

WriteGirl College and Alumnae Interns
Jennifer Ayuso
Dulce Castrejon
Jillian Davis
Wendy Garcia
Nell Gram
Yamuna Haroutunian
Angelica Hooper
DeAndria Milligan
Netta Rotstein
Lauren Sarazen
Greer Silverman

High School Interns
Camille Crisostomo
Joanna Cruz
Maribel Diaz
Alison Feinswog
Mari Flores
Diana Guzman
Myra Hollis
Rebecca Juan
Jazmine Mendoza
Myrtha Ortiz
Olivia Spitz
Kari Vides

THE WRITEGIRL "ENGINE"

Special thanks to the Constitutional Rights Foundation and New Village Charter High School for placement of teen interns with WriteGirl.

Event Planning
Special thanks to Jessica McCarthy for 2012-13 event management.

Website, Branding, Book Design, Graphics
Sara Apelkvist, Velvette De Laney, Nathalie Gallmeier, Juliana Sankaran-Felix

Photography/Videography
Lisa Beebe, Lindsay Boyce, Katie Geyer, Clayton Goodfellow, Thomas Hargis, Margaret Hyde, Mario de Lopez, Marie Nguyen, Sarah Waldorf, Marvin Yan

WriteGirl Board:

Advisory Board

Community Connections

Participating Schools

Alliance Gertz-Ressler High School

Albert Einstein Academy

Alverno High School

American Martyrs School

Arcadia High School

Aspire Pacific Academy

Beverly Hills High School

Bolsa Grande High School

Bravo Medical Magnet High School

Brentwood High School

Brethren Christian Schools

Bright Star Secondary Charter Academy

Burbank High School

California Virtual Academy at Los Angeles

Canyon High School

Cesar Chavez Learning Academies

CHAMPS Charter High School of the Arts

Chatsworth High School

Cheviot Hills High School

Chino Hills High School

Claremont High School

Culver City High School

Daniel Pearl Magnet High School

Downey High School

Eagle Rock High School

El Segundo Middle School

Fairfax High School

Flintridge Preparatory School

Foothill Country Day School

Frederick Douglass Academy

Garden Grove High School

Garvey Junior High School

Glen Wilson High School

Granada Hills Charter High School

Hamilton High School

Hamilton High School Academy of Music

Harbor Teacher Preparation Academy

Harvard-Westlake School

Huntington Beach High School

Immaculate Heart High School

International Studies Learning Center

John Burroughs Middle School

John Marshall High School

John Muir Middle School

King Drew Magnet High School
    of Medicine and Science

Los Angeles Center For Enriched Studies

Los Angeles High School

Los Angeles Unified Alternative
    Education School

Manhattan Beach High School

Mark Keppel High School

Mark Twain Middle School

Marlborough School

Marymount High School

Miguel Contreras Learning Complex

Mira Costa High School

Mira Loma High School

New Designs Charter School

New Roads High School

New Village Charter School

North Hollywood High School

Opportunities for Learning

Orchard Hills High School

Pacific Coast High School

Pacifica Christian High School

Palisades Charter High School

Pasadena High School

Port of Los Angeles High Schools

Providence High School

Robert F. Kennedy Community Schools
San Fernando Valley High School
Santa Fe Middle School
Santa Monica High School
South Hills High School
South Pasadena High School
Southern California Online Academy
South East High School
St. Bernard High School
St. Lucy's Priory High School
St. Mary's Academy
St. Paul Middle School

Summit View West School
Temple City High School
The Archer School for Girls
The Linden Center
Torrance High School
University High School
Venice High School
Westlake High School
Whittier High School
Wildwood School
Woodward High School

Referring Organizations:

Antioch University Los Angeles
Constitutional Rights Foundation
Fox Gives
Idealist
Los Angeles Times Festival of Books
Occidental College
PEN Center USA West
UCLA Extension Writers' Program
United Way of Ventura
VolunteerMatch
West Hollywood Book Fair
Writers Guild of America, West

WriteGirl Supporters

WriteGirl would like to thank the following for their generous support:

3 Arts Entertainment, Inc.

Barbara Abercrombie

Adams Family Foundation

The Ahmanson Foundation

Amazon.com

Jane Anderson

Annenberg Foundation

ASCAP

ASCAP Foundation

Band From TV

David Bonderman

Jean Bonini

Aline Brosh McKenna

California Community Foundation

Capital Group

Chernin Family Foundation

Chromatic, Inc.

Cinetic

City of Los Angeles Department of Cultural Affairs, Youth Arts Division

Community Partners

Elizabeth Craft

Crail-Johnson Foundation

Creative Artists Agency

Jennifer Crittenden

Danielle Laporte, Inc.

Susan Dickes

DirecTV Matching Gifts

Disney Ears to You/Entertainment Industry Foundation

Dwight Stuart Youth Fund

Edlow Family Fund

The Eisner Foundation

Sarah Fain

Fox Group

Fur Ball Inc.

Gap, Inc.

The Gernert Company

The Gersh Agency

Girl Friday Films, Inc.

Good News Foundation

Good Works Foundation

Green Foundation

Elizabeth Forsythe Hailey

Hansen, Jacobson, Teller, Hoberman,
    Newman, Warren, Richman,
    Rush & Kaller, L.L.P

HBK Investments

Margaret Hyde

International Pole Convention

JR Hyde III Family Foundation

Elizabeth Kruger

Last Punch Productions

Gigi Levangie

Lionsgate

Little, Brown and Company

Los Angeles County Office of Education

Christina Lynch

Marc & Eva Stern Foundation

Marlborough Student Charitable Fund of
    the Women's Foundation of California

Mule Design Studio

NBC Universal

Oder Family Foundation

Pacific Life Foundation

Partizan

Ralph M. Parsons Foundation

Ralphs (Kroger)

Reading Opens Minds

Ilene Resnick

Resnick Family Foundation

Lindy Robbins

Roll International

RR Donnelley

Rose Hills Foundation

Scripps Howard Foundation

Skirball Foundation

State Street Foundation

Eva Stern

Twentieth Century Fox Film
    Corporation

The UCLA Extension Writer's Program

United Talent Agency

Weingart Foundation

William Morris Endeavor

Lona Williams

Writer's House Literary Agency

Women Helping Youth

WriteGirl Supporters Cont.

Special thanks to Erica Jamieson for her generosity and continued support. In addition to volunteering with WriteGirl, Erica held a successful literary fundraiser for WriteGirl. A very special thank you to the following who contributed their words, goods or services – without them, the event would not have been nearly as wonderful:

Food-LA
Golden Road Brewery
John Montgomery
Kaleco Design
The Parlor
Pharmacie/Talmadge Lowe
Robert Daly
Shindig Events
Silver Lining Photos by Kim
Solomon, Saltsman & Jamieson
Stan's Donuts

Our Special Thanks to

All of our individual donors who have so generously contributed to help WriteGirl grow and help more teen girls each year.

All of WriteGirl's mentors and volunteers for professional services, including strategic planning, public relations, event coordination, mentoring management, training and curriculum development, catering, financial management and administrative assistance.

Advisory Board Members for their support and guidance on strategy, fundraising, communications and development of community partnerships.

Former Los Angeles Mayor Antonio Villaraigosa, The Honorable Mayor Eric Garcetti, Los Angeles City Council members Tom LaBonge and Jan Perry; for their support and acknowledgement of WriteGirl's contributions to the community.

Miguel Contreras Learning Complex, *Los Angeles Times* **Headquarters, The National Center for the Preservation of Democracy, Mark Taper Auditorium** at the **Los Angeles Central Public Library, Walt Disney Concert Hall, The Autry Museum, Petersen Automotive Museum, Linwood Dunn Theater** at the **Academy of Arts and Sciences** for providing workshop space where over 150 women and girls gathered to write each month; and **The Eli and Edythe Broad Stage** and the **Writers Guild of America** for event space.

Factory Place Arts Complex for volunteer trainings, editing workshops and college workshops space.

Los Angeles Times **Festival of Books, Skylight Books,** the **West Hollywood Book Fair** and the **UCLA Writers Faire** for donating WriteGirl space and promotional support at these events.

Sara Apelkvist for design and branding strategy, including development of the WriteGirl's logo, website, book design, press kit, stationery, publications and ongoing support. www.apelkvist.com

Los Angeles Unified School District—Beyond the Bell Division and **Google Inc.** for workshop and project supplies.

Writing Journals: Anne McGilvray & Company, Ariel Fox, Bee Healthy Candles, Blick Art Materials, Book Factory, BrushDance Inc., Carolina Pads, Cavallini Papers & Co., Chronicle Books, Ecojot, Edward Brothers Malloy, Falling Water, Fiorentina, Flavia, Galison/MudPuppy Press, Harry Abrams, Hartley and Marks, JournalBooks, Kikkerland Design, Michael Roger Press, Mirage Paper Company, Madison Park Group, Paperblanks, Quotable Cards, Retired Hipster, Rock Scissor Paper, Running Rhino & Co., K. Schweitzer, Studio 503, Trends International, USA Custom Pad Corp., Whimsy Press., Whitelines

Food, Dessert and Beverages at WriteGirl Workshops and Special Events: Angel City Brewery, Barefoot Wine & Bubbly, Big Sugar Bakeshop, Brooklyn Bagel Bakery, Butterbake Bakery, Cafe Dulce, Canelé, Carol Martin Cupcakes, Chipotle, Cookie Casa, Corner Bakery, Dave's Chillin & Grillin, Earth Wind and Flour, El Pollo Loco, Federal Brewing Company, Four Leaf, Frankie's on Melrose, Heath & Lejeune Inc., Homeboy Industries, Homegirl Cafe, IZZE Beverages, Kychon Chicken, La Pizza Loca, Les Macarons Duverger, Little Caesars Pizza, Little Dom's, Louise's Trattoria, Mani's Bakery, Masa of Echo Park, Mayura Indian Restaurant, Michael's Restaurant, Mozza, Musso and Franks, Nestlé Juicy Juice, Nickel Diner, Numero Uno Pizza, Olive Garden, Panda Restaurant Group, Panera Bread, Paper or Plastik Cafe, Paramount Farms, Pescado Mojado, Platine Cookies, POM Wonderful, P.O.P. Candy, Porto's Bakery, Pretzel Crisps, Ralphs, Sharky's Woodfired Mexican Grill, Spitz, Starbucks, Superior Nut Company, SusieCakes, The Riverside Café, TRU Vodka, Tom Bergin's Tavern, Tudor House, Uncle Eddies Vegan Cookies, Veggie Grill, Whole Foods Market, Yuca's and all of our volunteers who donated delicious desserts.

Gifts for Members and Special Events: ABC Family, ASCAP, Bambola Beauty, Barry's Boot Camp, Benefit Cosmetics, Boot Camp LA, Casa Del Mar, Cathy Waterman Inc., CG+Co., Daisy Rock Guitar, DIRECTV, Dr. Bronner's, Earthly Body, Earthpack, Evan Healy Cosmetics, Exhale Mind Body Spa, FACE Stockholm, FedEx Office, Finders Key Purse, Fox Gives, Fox Home Entertainment, Fox Searchlight, Get Fresh, Glee Gum, Granta, Hint Mints, iRobot Corporation, Justine Magazine, KINeSYS, KPR, Makeup Mandy, Margaret Hyde Photography, Marvin Yan Photography, MOCA, Mo's Nose, My Blankee, NBC Universal, NYX Cosmetics, Parlux Fragrances Inc., Porter Kelly Comedy, Quotable Cards, Roclord Studio Photography, Salon Benjamin, Soolip Paperie, Teleflora, The Good Cheer Company, The GRAMMY Museum, Two's Company, Wells Fargo, Wonderful Pistachios, Yogi Tea.

Printing and Copy Services: Chromatic, Inc., FedEx Office, RR Donnelley.

Meet the WriteGirl Mentors

Maia Akiva is a self-help writer. If you would like some help with yourself check her out at: www.maiaakiva.com.

Alisa Driscoll is an Orange County, CA native and fiction writer. She earns her paycheck as the MarComm Maven for a national nonprofit organization focused on the rights of girls. Driscoll enjoys reading, photography and catching typos from around the world.

Suzan Alparslan has had poems published in several print and online journals. She holds an MFA from Antioch University. She is currently working on a series of personal essays and is continually inspired by her magnificent mentee, Julia.

Jane Anderson is an award-winning screenwriter, playwright and director whose films have appeared on both large and small screens and whose plays have been produced off-Broadway and in theaters around the country.

Abby Anderson is a screenwriter who has placed in the semi-finals of the Nicholl Fellowship. She was also a Writer-in-Residence at Hedgebrook in 2009. Her mentee Jessica - now 21! - is in her 3rd year at Cal State Fullerton, majoring in Screenwriting.

Carol Bathke has worked at Camp Scott in the RTS program for the past two years. "These girls are an amazing, challenging and grateful group with so much potential. I'm a more insightful and effective teacher for this experience."

Lisa Beebe blogs and writes personality quizzes for TeenNick.com. She's working on her first YA novel and loves writing weird short stories. Lisa is endlessly inspired by her mentee, Grace Ardolino, and can't wait until they're both published novelists.

Natasha Billawala believes everyone has a tale to tell. Working in television has been her passion, and she enjoys not only the writing of it, but also studying its history. Writing on the show *Everwood* remains her favorite experience. She also writes the blog *A Little TLC* at www.thelivingcourse.org/alittletlc.

Teresa Boyer is a former teacher for the hearing impaired who now teaches literature and composition at several universities. She is working on her PhD in English.

Geneva Broussard's passion is writing! She writes poetry, lyrics, music and creative nonfiction. It was her first year with WriteGirl and she volunteered in the In-Schools program. She says working with the girls was a life-altering experience.

Julie Buchwald is a Special Investigator for the Los Angeles Police Commission's Office of the Inspector General by day and a creative fiction writer by night. Due to the stressful nature of her job, Julie greatly enjoys her volunteer work with WriteGirl and feels especially proud of helping the girls with their college application essays.

Sabrina D. Campbell is a graduate of George Washington University. She has written freelance scripts for the Disney animated cartoon, *The Proud Family,* and the Nickelodeon show, *Just Jordan.* Sabrina currently has projects under consideration at Columbia Pictures and Lifetime.

Jessica Ceballos is a writer, photographer, musician, cultural wanderer and Oxy and FIDM alumna. She's been recognized by the City of Los Angeles for her work bringing literary arts to the community via two monthly readings. More info at www.jessicaceballos.com.

Kathleen Cecchin is an actor, director and writer, whose piece *Pinocchia* was recently selected as one of six best plays in PlayGround LA's inaugural season. She is currently in preproduction of her short film *Pam*, to be shot this summer.

Marissa Christiansen earned her Masters in Urban Planning from USC. She lives in Los Angeles and loves every minute of it. She works in local government, volunteers with WriteGirl and Freedom & Fashion, and considers writing a paramount creative outlet.

Cindy Collins has a degree in journalism and a background in television production. She writes short stories, scripts and Web content, and participates in the grant writing process for her favorite nonprofit, WriteGirl.

Jody Cohan is an award-winning writer. Her current project is co-writing producer/director Doug Wilson's memoir about the people and places he encountered while spanning the globe with ABC Sports for 50 years. Jody also teaches writing at IvyMax Academy.

Irene Daniel is an estate planning attorney and writer who has been a WriteGirl volunteer since 2003. Originally from Arizona, Irene now lives in Eagle Rock with her husband and black lab, Maggie.

Tracy DeBrincat is the prize-winning author of a novel (*Hollywood Buckaroo*, Black Lawrence Press), two short story collections (*Troglodyte*, Elixir Press, January 2014, and *Moon Is Cotton & She Laugh All Night*, Subito Press) and the blog *Bigfoot Lives!* www.tracydebrincat.com.

Vicky Deger, originally from Australia, lives in Los Angeles where she works, runs, writes, surfs and contemplates the vast expense of tattoo removal. Her short life-based stories have appeared in *The Coachella Review, The Grove Review, Gulf Stream Magazine* and *Ducts*.

Loraine Despres is a best-selling novelist: *The Scandalous Summer of Sissy LeBlanc* and a recovering screenwriter: *Who Shot J.R.?*

Rachel Fain is a freelance writer, editor and organizer, as well as the Managing Director of LA StoryWorks and the LA Storytelling Festival. She has been active in Los Angeles theater production and education for nearly 20 years. www.rachelgfain.com; www.lastagetimes.com/author/rachelfain/

Sarah Thomas Fazeli writes for XOJANE.COM and has an MFA from CalArts. She is also a performer, and is thrilled to be exploring poetry, a brand new genre for her!

Laura Ferguson has a PhD from UCLA in American film and literature. She writes and produces documentaries and teaches many ages and classes in Los Angeles. She lives in Hollywood with her husband and varying numbers of their four children.

Susanne Ferrull is an editor, journalist, publicist and freelance writer focusing primarily on entertainment and travel.

Linda Folsom, a volunteer with WriteGirl for five years, has had the honor of working with two excellent mentees. She attributes completing her YA novel to the energy she gets being around the talented women of WriteGirl.

Almost ten years ago, **Glenda Garcia** was a WriteGirl mentee. WriteGirl nominated Glenda for a Posse Foundation full-tuition scholarship to Dickinson College. She went on to graduate from college and serve her country through AmeriCorps VISTA and later was awarded a Fulbright Fellowship to Thailand. Today, Glenda is a WriteGirl Operations Coordinator.

Kim Genkinger is an advertising Creative Director at Fire Station Agency. Over the past five years she has been focused on the discipline of creating big campaign ideas that help drive big sales along with big laughs. Kim has written and produced award-winning commercials for clients including Wonderful Pistachios, Cuties Clementines, POM Wonderful and Teleflora.

Katie Geyer is trying to prove that cowgirls can be writers, too. She grew up on a horse ranch and then studied at UCLA and Boston University to become a political reporter. She alternates listening to NPR and country music.

A seasoned curriculum developer, **Kirsten Giles** joined WriteGirl as their Workshops Coordinator in 2009. Kirsten writes poetry, nonfiction/self-help, and loves to create new writing experiments for the amazing women and girls of WriteGirl. Kirsten also owns and operates Pale Blue Design, a training company that serves the automotive industry.

Corrie Greathouse, a reformed relocator recently featured by KCET as one of the "Iconic Women in Literary LA," is the author of the novella *"Another Name for Autumn,"* a Twitter enthusiast, *whom* advocate, and fan of the Oxford Comma.

Karin Heard's career was 40 years as an elementary school teacher. When retired she joined the Pasadena Humane Society to do pet therapy. She later became a docent for the Los Angeles Zoo to tour students and do Outreach in the schools for Special Needs students to become acquainted with animals.

A television and film development executive, **Anna Henry** reads stacks of scripts and books, watches tons of TV, and works with award-winning screenwriters to guide and improve their projects. She's not a "writer," but she writes a lot, every day!

Connie K. Ho is a Freelance Contributor for online publications. Her work has appeared in AOL *Patch, The Orange County Register, the Pacific Citizen, Mochi Magazine* and *Red Orbit*. Reach her on Twitter at the handle @conniekho.

Teresa Huang is a genuine graduate of MIT who gave up problem sets and thermo-dynamics to become a writer, actor and producer. Her super powers include power napping, parallel parking and spending too much money at farmer's markets.

Ashaki M. Jackson is a social psychologist, writer and foodie living in Los Angeles. Her work is available in publications by *Eleven Eleven, Suisun Valley Review, Cave Canem* and others. She runs to Radiohead and Trinidad James in her downtime.

Janet Alston Jackson, author of *A Cry for Light: A Journey into Love*, winner of the National USA Book News Award for Christian Inspiration, is a keynote speaker and teaches Mindfulness Based Stress Management for companies and organizations.

Erica W. Jamieson's work has been honored with awards and published online and in print. She has short fiction upcoming in *Lilith Magazine* and *R.kv.r.y. Quarterly Literary Journal.* She will travel far and wide for a good cup of coffee, an artisan pizza and to work with the girls from WriteGirl who teach her weekly that every story is a gift to the reader! She lives in Los Angeles with her husband, two children and a whoodle named Willa.

Kat Kambes is a poet, fiction-writer, playwright and journalist. Her work has been published in *Short and Deadly, Citron Review, 2005 Best Poets* and *Skive's Americana Issue*, to name a few. Her play, *Strindberg In Love*, was produced in L.A.

Rachel McLeod Kaminer is completing a book of poetry and a master's degree this year. A former wilderness field instructor, she's done a lot of her growing up in the Appalachians. She's noticed the average WriteGirl is a total delight AND a genius. What are the odds!?

LaCoya Katoe is a graduate of Lake Forest College (BA) and Antioch University-Los Angeles (MFA). Her primary focus is Black Women's Literature. For the past six years she has facilitated book groups and writing workshops for young adults in alternate school programs in Chicago, IL. LaCoya is currently editing her short story collection, and at work on a new novel.

Porter Kelly is an actor and comedy writer. She wrote and performed at ACME Comedy Theatre for seven years. TV acting credits include *The Office, Private Practice, New Girl* and many others. Stage credits range from *Shakespeare to Sondheim*, and she has appeared in over 40 commercials.

Retta Putignano King is the head writer at Create Your Reel, a company she co-owns, and she has written over 3,500 scenes for actors' reels. She divides her writing time between a romance novel, an action screenplay and a comedy web series.

Kendra Kozen is an award-winning journalist whose work appears in print and online. A native New Yorker, she holds a master's degree from the University of Southern California and has called Los Angeles home for more than a decade.

Elline Lipkin is a poet, nonfiction writer and academic. She loves learning new words, working on her writing, and spending time with her family, friends and elderly cat. Her book of poems, *The Errant Thread*, was published in 2006.

Christina Lynch is a television writer, journalist and writing instructor, and is co-author with Meg Howrey under the pseudonym Magnus Flyte of *City of Dark Magic* and *City of Lost Dreams*. She lives near Sequoia National Park.

Reparata Mazzola is a published author, a produced screenwriter and an Emmy nominated writer/producer. As a member of Barry Manilow's back-up trio, Lady Flash, she recorded seven of his albums, two TV specials and toured the world. Currently, she has two films in development.

Amy McGranahan works as an assistant at RAND, and enjoys editing documents. She is finishing her master's thesis on mood and anxiety, and is a contributing writer for *Astonish* magazine. She has written conference papers on narcissism, authoritarianism, stigma and competition.

Chelsey Monroe is a novelist, producer and wardrobe stylist. She's written three books, produced over 15 short films and currently works as a freelance stylist in the commercial business. She graduated valedictorian from UCLA with degree in theater.

Maria Angelica Narciso, aka Just JillN, is a former newspaper journalist, part-time freelancer and full-time obsessor of words, graphic novels, movies, *Gizzelle the Model*, *Babie Draper* and *Mico Rico Azul*.

Sandra Ramos O'Briant is the author of *The Sandoval Sisters' Secret of Old Blood* (La Gente Press, 2012). A complete listing of her published short stories and excerpts from her novel can be found at www.thesandovalsisters.com.

Sheana Ochoa, writer, feminist, mother, has learned from experience that change happens one minute, one girl at a time. Her forthcoming biography *Stella Adler: A Life in Art* chronicles the life a woman who forfeited family life for her art.

Carly Pandza was a 4th grade novelist who filled up her journals and numbered the pages. An avid artist activist, this summer she is leading a group of students in Africa to create a social entrepreneurship in a rural village through the company ThinkImpact.

Blazhia Parker enjoys writing free verse and imagist poetry.

Kathy Peterson is a mother of a mentee and very proud that she is involved with WriteGirl! "Happy to help wherever I can for I truly believe this organization changes lives for the better in so many ways."

Hunter Phillips is a writer, director, producer and principal at Free Radical Pictures. The young women of WriteGirl are a source of inspiration, levity and wit that Hunter continues to appreciate. She is honored to be a WriteGirl mentor.

India Radfar is a poet with four published books of poetry and one chapbook. She teaches for California Poets-in-the-Schools and The Creative Minds Project out of UCLA, and she is becoming a Certified Applied Poetry Facilitator with the National Federation for Bibilo/Poetry Therapy. She loves volunteering for the WriteGirl In-Schools Program.

Anne Ramallo writes about design, business, healthcare, technology, innovation and literature. Working with leaders in these fields, she makes their thoughts and ideas accessible and engaging to wide audiences. She's the author of *Outdoor Rooms II* and currently the Manager of Communications at Karten Design.

Diahann Reyes is a nonfiction writer, a blogger and an actor. She is working on a memoir. Before becoming an artist, she was a CNN writer/producer, a public relations account manager and the first executive editor of *FindLaw*. Visit www.DiahannReyes.com.

Emily Richmond loves every aspect of WriteGirl, from mentoring at workshops to working with incarcerated girls. When she's not writing, she shops at farmers' markets, runs and dances her heart out...and then goes home to write about it.

Liz Rizzo directs short films and web content, works in post production and blogs like it's 2005. An FSU Film School grad, her short, *Zero Sight: Bad Call* will air on Stage 5 TV's YouTube show *The Continuum* in 2013.

Monice Mitchell Simms is a published author and authorpreneur, who enjoys volunteering, speaking and teaching – not necessarily in that order. She recently published her debut novel, *Address: House of Corrections* – the first in a trilogy inspired by the lives of her grandmother, mother and great-grandmother.

Inez Singletary, author of *Making What Your Means Can't Buy*, an exploration into how to make connections to both survive and thrive and are not dependent on money. She enjoys making art and loves writing astrological guidance in her blog.

Kristie Soares is a PhD candidate in Comparative Literature at the University of California, Santa Barbara. She is also a performance poet, and is one half of the bi-coastal performance poetry duo, GUAPA.

Marilee Stefenhagen, retired public library administrator, dreams of returning to the library to host a Children's Storytime featuring her published books. A Soroptimist member, she enjoys mentoring teens and encouraging them to live their dreams.

Jacqueline Steiger is an actress, writer, tutor and gung-ho nerd. She graduated from UCLA with a BA in linguistics and anthropology (which means she has a degree in funny words) and a minor in LGBT studies. She also works at Comic Con.

Gabrielle Toft is a writer from a small town in northern California. She has been published in several important things. She teaches English and lives in Los Angeles, in a loft, with her boyfriend and their two cats. WriteGirl has changed her life.

Marie Unini helps people buy and sell real estate. She lives in the mountains with two horses, a nutty-creative husband Robert, and many creatures wild and domestic, including the scrub jay who has trained them to feed him peanuts.

Kristen Waltman has been Guadalupe Mendoza's mentor for the last three seasons of WriteGirl and has been a volunteer since 2010. Kristen works as a ghostwriter and social media manager at a branded entertainment agency called Brand Arc.

Melanie Zoey Weinstein is a playwright, screenwriter and actress. Her plays have been performed off-Broadway and in festivals throughout the country. Her short film *I'm Sorry* will be coming soon to a YouTube near you. UCLA Professional Program in Screenwriting 2013. WRITE, GIRLS!

Maiya Williams is a Television Writer and Producer whose credits include *Fresh Prince of Bel Air, Mad TV* and *Futurama*. She is also a writer of children's novels. A volunteer for two years, she thinks the world of WriteGirl!

Jessica Williams wholeheartedly believes nurturing and dedication to one's creativity invites an enthusiastic and courageous approach to life! Hailing from sunny California, a writer and a righter! Daughter, friend, aunt who hopes to be a great mother someday!

Melissa Wong is a television writer living in Los Angeles. Her credits include *The 63rd Annual Emmy Awards* and *The MTV Movie Awards*. She currently writes for NBC's hit show *The Voice*. This is her 6th year as a WriteGirl mentor.

"How much the girls encourage each other is inspiring"

— WriteGirl Parent

Index

W

X

Y

Z

About The Publisher / Editors

Keren Taylor, Executive Director of WriteGirl, has been a community leader for nearly two decades. In 2001, she founded WriteGirl with the idea of leveraging the skills of women writers to mentor underserved youth through a slate of creative writing workshops, one-on-one mentoring and college readiness programs. Under Keren's direction, WriteGirl has become a recognized and lauded innovator in youth arts education in Los Angeles, building unique partnerships with leading civic and cultural organizations.

Committed to providing a cutting edge approach to learning and creativity, Keren and the WriteGirl leadership draw from many different fields and backgrounds to design dynamic programing to reach girls of widely disparate learning levels and engage even the most reticent learner. For 11 years, WriteGirl has guided 100% of the high school seniors in its Core Mentoring Program to graduate from high school and enroll in college.

Working with a team of editors and designers, Keren has directed the production of over two dozen anthologies of writing by teen girls and their mentors. To date, WriteGirl publications have been awarded 55 national and international book awards.

Keren has overseen WriteGirl's expansion into a thriving community of women and teen writers and an organization that helps hundreds of Los Angeles girls annually. In 2010, WriteGirl was awarded a Medal for Service and named the 2010-2011 California Nonprofit of the Year by Governor Arnold Schwarzenegger and First Lady Maria Shriver. WriteGirl also received the 2010 HUMANITAS Philanthropy Prize and was a finalist in the 2011 National Arts & Humanities Youth Program Awards.

Passionate about helping women and girls, Keren is a popular speaker at conferences and book festivals nationwide, including the Association of Writing Programs Annual Conference, BOOST Conference, *Los Angeles Times* Festival of Books and Guiding Lights Festival. Keren has led staff development workshops for the California Paraeducator Conference, California School-Age Consortium, California Department of Education, Los Angeles County Office of Education, LA's BEST and the New York Partnership for After School Education, among others. Keren has been selected to serve as a Community Champion and facilitator for the Annenberg Foundation's Alchemy Program, helping guide nonprofit leaders to organizational success.

Keren is the recipient of numerous awards and accolades, including the President's Volunteer Call to Service Award, Business & Professional Women's Community Woman of Achievement Award, Soroptimist International's Woman of Distinction Award, commendations from Los Angeles Mayor Antonio Villaraigosa and others.

Keren is an assemblage artist and mosaicist. She holds a Bachelor's Degree in International Relations from the University of British Columbia, a Piano Performance Degree from the Royal Conservatory of Music, Toronto and a Diploma from the American Music and Dramatic Academy, New York City.

Announcing the Honorees at the 2012 WriteGirl Bold Ink Awards.

Keren Taylor at Walt Disney Concert Hall for the 12th annual WriteGirl Songwriting Workshop.

Allison Deegan serves as WriteGirl's Associate Director and has provided critical strategic and operational guidance since the organization's inception in 2001. She participates in all aspects of WriteGirl's leadership, programming and sustainability, and also serves on the WriteGirl Advisory Board. Professionally, Allison is a fiscal and policy coordinator with the Los Angeles County Office of Education, where she works on a variety of projects including the development of the Road to Success Academy, a successful new project-based learning school for incarcerated girls. She has made numerous presentations around the country on topics related to after school program success, creative writing and working with youth. She is a mentor, trainer and curriculum consultant with the California School-Age Consortium, which provides professional development to after school program staff. She holds a B.S. in Marketing from Syracuse University, a Master's Degree in Public Policy from California State University, Long Beach (CSULB) and a Doctorate in Educational Leadership, also from CSULB. Allison is a screenwriter and fiction writer and has remained close to her WriteGirl mentee, who is currently in graduate school.

About WriteGirl

www.writegirl.org

Founded in 2001, WriteGirl is a creative writing and mentoring organization that promotes creativity, critical thinking and leadership skills to empower teen girls. Through its Core Mentoring and In-Schools Programs, WriteGirl serves over 300 at-risk teen girls in Los Angeles County. The Core Mentoring Program pairs at-risk teen girls from more than 60 schools with professional women writers for one-on-one mentoring, workshops, internships and college admission and scholarship guidance. Mentee-mentor pairs meet at coffee shops, libraries and other creatively inspiring locations. Creative writing workshops are held at prestigious cultural and civic institutions such as Walt Disney Concert Hall, the Autry Museum and the Academy of Motion Picture Arts and Sciences' Linwood Dunn Theater. For eleven years, WriteGirl has guided 100% of girls in the Core Mentoring Program to not only graduate from high school but also enroll in college. *YOU ARE HERE: The WriteGirl Journey* is the 12th anthology from WriteGirl.

The WriteGirl In-Schools Program brings creative writing mentors into the classroom at schools all over Los Angeles County. Students at these schools are pregnant or parenting teens, foster youth, on probation, assigned to social workers or facing significant other challenges. Curriculum is standards-based and adaptable for a wide variety of populations. In 2011, with support from the Los Angeles County Office of Education, WriteGirl launched a 24-week creative writing program for incarcerated teens at the Road to Success Academy, serving two detention camps in Santa Clarita. In 2012, WriteGirl successfully guided a 12-week series of workshops in Peru under the name *Escriba Chica*.

Through participation in WriteGirl, students develop vital communication skills, self-confidence, critical thinking skills, deeper academic engagement and enhanced creativity for a lifetime of increased opportunities.

Every word counts.